SONS OF BARBEE COLLINS

Sons of Barbee Collins

William See

ISBN-13: 9780692926932
ISBN-10: 0692926933
Library of Congress Control Number: 2017911734
William A. See III, Frankewing, TENNESSEE

Acknowledgements

———◆———

I MUST THANK MY PARENTS, Billy and Vickie See for their help and encouragement. I also must thank my family, Danielle, William, and Lauren for their patience. I also appreciate my great-great-great-great-great-great-great-grand father, Barbe Collins, for inspiring certain components of the story. I thank Josh Smith for the illustrations and proofreading. I also appreciate Ashley and Mary Beth for proofreading.

CHAPTER 1

A ROAD TRIP

———◆———

WYATT MASHBURN LOOKED INTO THE mirror of an empty truck-stop restroom and said, "You've shit your pants, you idiot." He continued to stare into the mirror. His hair was unkempt and slept upon. His gray T-shirt was stained and ill fitting. He thought he looked like a bum. Now, with shit in his pants, he felt like a bum. He walked into a stall. Starting with his shoes, he began removing his layers one at a time. He delicately ascertained what was salvageable. Wyatt handled this with as much grace as could be expected. He took a leave-no-trace approach, out of respect for the truck stop. He cleaned himself with wet paper towels and soap, and was able to save his clothes—except for his underwear; those he left in the trashcan.

He finished the chore and policed the stall. He felt his pockets to make sure he had his wallet and pocket knife. He opened the stall and went back to the mirror. He then gave his gawking reflection in the mirror a "Yeah, what of it?" face. He walked out into the parking lot. Walking awkwardly due to his new commando status, he came to his pickup truck. In it sat Maggie Fields. He walked up to Maggie's side and stretched like a cockerel. Her window was down as she pretended to be waiting patiently. Like a grand, stoic statesman, he said calmly, "No problems." Maggie howled with laughter. She could hold it no more. "No problems besides the shit in your pants!" Wyatt pretended to ignore it as he got back behind the wheel.

After getting back onto the interstate, Maggie wasn't laughing as much and began to calm down a bit. She conspicuously arranged a bag of pork skins and a jar of pickled eggs on the middle seat as if they were a creature to be reckoned with. Suddenly she straightened up, waved her hand in a gesture like one of Barker's Beauties, and said to Wyatt, "Care for some more?"

"No, thanks."

Maggie resumed her obnoxious and now contrived laughter.

Wyatt and Maggie had known each other for nearly two years but had only been a couple a few months. Maggie was nothing to look at. She was pale and overfed. She gave her mousy hair little attention. Her glasses were overly large and outdated, when she wore them. She kept no makeup, and she could be awkwardly bashful at times. It was her dry wit that first interested Wyatt, but her shyness and plainness did not kindle much attraction.

Wyatt was still humiliated after the episode. While he drove, Maggie smirked as she knew he was feigning coolness to save face. Wyatt felt gross and foul. He did not want to think of Maggie now, but he did. Right then he thought of her silliness. He found her tendency to laugh crude humor annoying, especially now that it was at his expense. He wished he were somewhere else. He felt as if a shell of filth were enveloping him, and Maggie was part of it. These thoughts and her picking at him made him more frustrated with her. He felt she should do more to help herself, and she had some nerve to laugh at him. At that moment he regretted going on the trip. This particular trip had been his idea.

Wyatt had been mowing yards but was starting to hate it and needed a temporary escape. He mowed them for Mr. Robert MacAnally. Mr. MacAnally ran a lawn service of some size twenty years ago. At one time he had four drivers and mowed half the yards of Lincoln County, Tennessee. After the business became profitable, a large commercial outfit came in and bought the business. Mr. MacAnally then went into roofing. That was five years ago. But because folks in the area still thought of Mr. MacAnally as having a lawn service, they still called him. He used to apologize and tell them he had sold the business. This stopped most of the calls. After some years passed, he bought a fancy mower to cut his own holdings. He thought to create a small amount of side capital by hiring Wyatt to cut a handful of yards for older neighbors who still called. This manner of work suited Wyatt. The offer Mr. MacAnally gave him at the time sounded solid, and Wyatt took it. Now, however, he was tired of it. It generated enough to pay his utilities and cheap groceries but not much more. One evening in late summer, Wyatt and Maggie were sitting together on what they called the porch of their abode.

As he sat with Maggie, he said, "It's about time to go on a trip again."

"Why do you say that?" Maggie asked.

"Let's go camping and visiting."

"For how long?"

"I don't know—for a while."

Maggie pretended to act hesitant. "Will the truck make it?"

"Yes," said Wyatt. "I've got an uncle in Covington, apparently."

"Covington, Kentucky?"

"Yes, we could head that way and stay at parks."

"Ones with showers?"

"Yes."

"Have you ever met this uncle?

"No, but Cora did."

"How did your sister find him?"

"When she got married to Lawrence, I think. His parents helped her find some relatives to harass with wedding invitations. She must have found out about them through Justine."

"She met him?" Maggie asked.

"Yes, I think so. She said he was a curious type but old. He sent her a letter when he got the invitation. He said he had heard of us and wanted to meet us. I think he or his son even stopped by Cora and Lawrence's place in Illinois. She said he was very nice."

"Well, I guess we should. What's his name?"

"Luke, I think."

Neither of them had a legitimate reason for not wanting to go. Wyatt needed to be on the road for a while. He was still searching for his way. He needed a cause in which to lend his passion, one that could push him past his laziness. Maggie was happy to be with Wyatt. She found him to be kind and patient and usually enjoyed his adventures. She did not have to talk much, and Wyatt got her sense of humor.

That night they slept with a trip on their minds, and both saw themselves hitting the road in a week or so. When the next morning came, Wyatt awoke chipper and after an hour said, "Let's load up!"

"Today?"

"Yep! Why not?"

Maggie had no reason to object, and began packing without comment.

They loaded the truck with a tent and sleeping necessities. Maggie filled a patched picnic basket with most of the food they had in the house. Wyatt also collected and brought a few hand tools. By noon they were ready to leave.

There was no rush to be anywhere and a few hours later were setting up camp at a state park in northern Middle Tennessee. Wyatt pitched the tent and arranged the sleeping bags while Maggie explored the shower house like a queen inspecting a new palace with her nose in the air.

They finished most of the items in the food basket and went to sleep early with their bellies full. The next morning was pleasant. They woke and finished off the foodstuff in the basket and headed north.

Something about driving straight to Covington and dropping in on his unknown uncle seemed awkward.

"Let's camp for a couple more days before we go see this Uncle Luke," he decided.

"That sounds good to me," said Maggie.

"Maybe I'll call Cora and see if she can tell him we are coming."

They drove a ways farther pulling into a large truck stop for gas and more snacks for the basket. As he walked toward the reflective doors of the truck stop, Wyatt saw his reflection. It caused him to grimace and straighten his posture. He walked into the restroom and relieved himself. Looking into the mirror, he washed his hands. He did not like what he saw. His was unshaven and scruffy. His pants were tight, although they had fit a month ago. He stared at two vacant slots in his mouth where he had lost two teeth from the upper left side two years ago. The reflection staring back at him was sloppy. He wanted to do something about it, but what? He dampened his hair with some water from the sink and proceeded to comb his hair with his fingers. He looked at the mirror once more and sighed with disappointment.

He walked out of the restroom now, looking for some snacks to replenish the basket that Maggie would like.

Another fleeting memory of the conversation he had just held in the restroom mirror made him decide to look for something healthy. "No sugar," he thought to himself. Then he saw what he was looking for: pickled eggs!

The eggs were in a half-gallon jar with a wide-mouth opening so a man could get his hand in easily. Wyatt thought their pinkish hue added to the appeal. The jar had a sticker that read, "Half price. Ten dollars."

Not only were these gems good for you as well as proteinaceous and practical, they were on sale! Wyatt grabbed the jar and placed it under his arm with an air of success. Next to them he saw a large bag of fried pork skins. "Score!" he thought as he grabbed the bag. Wyatt sat the eggs, pork skins, and a gallon jug of purified water on the counter to pay. He smiled heroically as he handed the clerk a twenty and thought of how interesting it would be when Maggie saw how practical and nutritious his selected items were.

He marched to the truck as if he were Napoleon carrying groceries. He walked up to Maggie's side and gestured for her to help him find a place in the center seat of the truck so the eggs and pork skins could be easily reached.

"That's what you got?" Maggie asked with mouth agape. She stared at Wyatt as he fumbled with the items. Maggie huffed and went back inside the gas station. She reemerged five minutes later with a sack of Bugles, two Dr. Peppers and an Almond Joy. She got back into the truck, looked at Wyatt with his eggs, and said, "You are going to be sick." Wyatt started on the eggs in defiance and started the pickup. He ate two eggs in the parking lot and finished a third as he accelerated back onto the interstate.

They drove north a little ways and saw signs for Mammoth Cave. Maggie liked the suggestion of checking it out, so they did.

"Let's stay here for a couple of days," said Wyatt.

"Sure, this looks nice," Maggie agreed.

They found a campground site that suited them, and set up their small camp to enjoy the evening. The sun glittered through the broad green leaves. The breeze was pleasant. Wyatt found some time to call Cora.

"Hey, Sis."

"Hey, Wyatt. How are you?"

"We're good. We have been camping."

"That sounds fun. Where are you?"

"We just crossed into Kentucky."

"Kentucky? We have family there. An uncle."

"That's what I was calling about. We may go see the one in Covington."

"Yes, there is Luke in Covington, but we also have one closer to where you are. I believe his name is Charlie."

"Charlie? I haven't heard of him."

"He sends out those Facebook messages to his family. He's an old man."

"I guess we could go see him."

"Yes, you should. He seems really nice."

"It seems weird to just drop in on them," said Wyatt.

"Well, call them first. Use your charm."

"I don't know. It seems too weird. They are going to think that we just want to mooch off of them or something."

"That's silly. I don't think they will feel that way. They probably feel a little sorry for us," she said.

"Would you call them for me, Cora?"

"I guess so, but why don't you do it?"

"I don't know. It just seems weird. Will you just call them, please?"

"Yes, but you are silly," said Cora.

"Thanks."

"When shall I tell them you will be there?"

"Sometime this weekend or later. I need the addresses."

She gave Wyatt the addresses she had. "Okay, y'all be careful," she said.

"We will. Thanks, Sis."

"No problem. Be careful, and I will see you later."

"Okay. See you. Bye."

They stayed at the campground around the cave for a couple of days until they were ready for a change of scenery. As they prepared to leave, Wyatt commented, "I was thinking we could go see this Uncle Charlie before we leave Kentucky. Cora said she was going to call him and tell him we were coming," said Wyatt.

"Sounds good. I wonder what he is like?" asked Maggie.

"Odd, probably. Most folks in my family are a little off."

Maggie giggled.

About an hour later, they arrived at Uncle Charlie's house. They got out and knocked on the door. A few minutes later, an ancient man answered. He opened a bolted door and stood facing Wyatt through the screen. The old man looked at Wyatt and said, "Can I help you?"

"Uncle Charlie, it's Wyatt, your great-nephew. We are just dropping in to say hello."

Charlie's face lit up. He remembered Cora's call, and realized this must be the brother she mentioned.

"Uncle Charlie, this is Maggie," said Wyatt.

"Hi, Maggie," Uncle Charlie said, with little true interest. "Come in. Come in."

Maggie and Wyatt went in and sat on a couch while Uncle Charlie sat across from them. They sat there politely while Charlie asked questions. Wyatt told him they were going on a trip to see various relatives. "We may even drive up and see Uncle Luke in Covington," said Wyatt.

He began telling Wyatt a few stories as old men do. Uncle Charlie laughed heartily as his own tales amused him. He also told Wyatt that Cora told him of the deaths of their father and brother. Charlie said he was sorry to hear it, and he hoped things would be better for them in the future.

Trying to be polite, and thinking of topics Uncle Charlie might find interesting, Wyatt asked him if he had read any good books lately. Charlie said he had not. Wyatt regretted asking the question. Charlie said his vision was poor, and it took him forever to read anything but he said he listened to the radio quite a bit.

"I do have a pretty good book collection though. Take a look," Charlie said, as he gestured for Wyatt to go and browse the shelves. To avoid rudeness, Wyatt did so and feigned interest. "Do you see anything you like?" asked Charlie.

"I'll look," said Wyatt. He stood in front of a shelf and examined its contents. There were old volumes on Bible study and many for plant and bird identification. Among some books of poetry was a tattered book in a sleeve. The gold lettering caught his eye. *Don Quixote*, it read. Wyatt recognized the name from a print of a Picasso painting bearing the same title that hung in his grandmother's hallway.

"That's a neat old copy of *Don Quixote* you've got there," said Wyatt.

"Ah, yes. It was your uncle's. He found it not long ago at a yard sale. He read it and put it there. Take it with you if you'd like," said Charlie.

Wyatt, sensing Charlie's lack of attachment to it, said, "Well, I might."

"Have you read *Don Quixote*?" asked Uncle Charlie.

"Nope."

"Good. Take it. It's hilarious."

Wyatt took the book off the shelf, looked at the outside briefly, and put it under his arm. He walked back to the couch next to Maggie. They continued to sit and make small talk with Charlie. Wyatt's apparent interest in old things pleased the old man.

After a while, Uncle Charlie told Wyatt about an old stamp collection he had. He said it once belonged to his brother, but it was all in a huge worthless mess now. He had hoped to give it to some resourceful young relative sometime, and

Wyatt was the perfect candidate. Charlie said it supposedly held some pieces of value once. He stood and said, "It will take me a few minutes to dig it out, but you make yourselves at home. While Charlie was digging in the closet, Wyatt went outside to stretch his legs and let off some gas. He walked over to the truck and got two more pickled eggs out of the jar and ate them.

"Delicious," he thought. "Why won't Maggie eat these?"

He walked back into the house. Uncle Charlie had produced an old leather suitcase that contained three leather binders. Inside each one was a conglomerate of small colored pieces of paper and glue that had once been a stamp collection.

"They are all stuck together. My brother Albert had collected these over many years. But during a move they got wet, I guess, and they glued themselves into a big mess. Albert was going to throw it all away, but instead he put them here."

Maggie and Wyatt both heard the story and looked at each other. He was not sure if they had room for them, nor did he want them. "What do you think should be done with them, Charlie?" asked Maggie.

"Sell the ones you can peel off and chuck the others," Charlie said and laughed, "no one else wants them." Charlie laughed more. Maggie perceived part of Charlie's laughter was due to the huge mess the stamps were in. Wyatt took the case and repeated three times to Uncle Charlie how much he appreciated the gift. The trio sat and talked a few minutes more.

"Will you have some tea before you go?" Charlie asked.

Maggie and Wyatt both welcomed the gesture, as they were thirsty. Wyatt was the thirstiest after his recent pickled eggs. They also were ready to head down the road and were glad Charlie had opened the opportunity for departure. Charlie poured chilled ice tea from the refrigerator into three small tumbler glasses. They sipped the tea like cordials.

After the exchange was over, Wyatt walked toward the door, carrying the old book and the suitcase containing the stuck-together stamp collection. Maggie gave Uncle Charlie a hug and followed Wyatt toward the truck. Wyatt thanked him once more for the stamps.

Charlie thanked them for the visit and said, "Come again any time."

Wyatt got into the truck and handed Maggie the suitcase of stamps.

"What in the hell are you going to do with these?" Maggie asked, once they were moving.

"Maybe they will come apart."

"I doubt it," said Maggie.

"They are junk, most likely. We will throw them away when we get home." Wyatt looked at her and smiled sarcastically as he continued to drive.

Still holding cheeky eye contact, he reached into the egg jar and grabbed two more. He shoved them into his mouth and devoured them while growling like a lion. Maggie looked down and noticed the jar was already half eaten. Again she glared at him, and again she said, "You're going to be sick."

Wyatt slowed and stopped for a stop sign. He revved the engine to signify the artificial energy the eggs had given him. Before accelerating, he grabbed a handful of the pork skins. He ate them with the same ceremony he gave to the eggs. After the gulp he let out a hugely satisfying belch for his captive audience of one. Maggie stared straight ahead with the expression of a prisoner who had just finished her day's torture. She pretended Wyatt was invisible.

In order to continue pretending to be unimpressed, Maggie picked up the case with the stamps inside and opened it. Wyatt continued to drive. Maggie got out the three binders. She cleaned off the outside of the binders with a rag she kept under her side of the truck seat. She wiped them off, looking for any label or writing and intentionally avoiding opening them for fear of the mess they contained. Finding no marks to satisfy her on the outside, she showily placed one of the binders on her lap and prepared to open it. She released an exaggerated sigh as she opened the first one. On top were a few loose pieces of paper, a few odd postcards, and a few extraneous loose stamps placed there by someone who had just found an odd stamp and did not know where else to put it. Those she collected, bunching them together in a stack, and then she set them aside. She sat quietly and stared at the remaining contents. Wyatt was obliged to drive, so he could not contribute to the effort, but he was curious about what she was finding.

"What do they look like?" he asked.

"They're a damn mess," she croaked.

Wyatt reached over to ascertain how firmly they were attached to one another. The one he tried tore slightly with the gentle tug.

Maggie slapped his had away. "You'll have to steam them," she said.

"Steam them?" Wyatt asked. "Is it worth it?"

"Hell, no!"

Wyatt said nothing else as Maggie began putting the binders back into the case. Wyatt continued to drive. While Maggie pretended to be frustrated with the stamps, she was secretly enjoying the adventure. She liked seeing Wyatt show hints of ambition. She enjoyed being an out-of-towner. She felt more grandiose as an outsider, and she sat up a little straighter and deemphasized her accent unintentionally when she went through a different town and came in view of its inhabitants. She was frequently embarrassed at how she looked when she saw herself in the passenger-side mirror. She knew she needed to fix her hair and grab some makeup, but it wasn't convenient, and she lacked the supplies. Her teeth were gray in places due to decay as a child. She wanted to fix these problems that she thought were temporary, but she lacked the funds and motivation.

After a while some of the gas from the eggs and pork skins reached Wyatt's lower bowels. He was going to seize this opportunity to build upon his previous alpha-male demonstrations to Maggie. After careful calculation, he felt the timing was optimal. With great pomp and display, Wyatt postured like a great ape and beat upon his chest and made leering faces at Maggie. She continued to pretend he was invisible. Wyatt assumed a position, lifted his right butt cheek, and proceeded to produce a sonorous fart. The first two seconds of the event went as Wyatt planned. A tubalike tone of good volume and sustain was coming out of Wyatt. Impressed with the racket, he strained to increase its effect on the listener. This did change the tone to that of pudding being extruded under pressure. Upon this change, Wyatt clamped down to abort the fart. He froze for a moment, allowing his senses to sort out the situation. Maggie also froze and looked straight ahead. She still pretended he was invisible but was also trying her best to hold back laughter.

Without much ado, Wyatt signaled and took the next exit ramp. He headed toward the sign of a truck stop without comment, and his faced bore no expression. He pulled into a parking space in front of the building instead of at the gas pump, implying he was going to be a while. He opened the truck door and got out. He walked into the truck stop with short strides, all the while pretending to Maggie that nothing had happened. Wyatt walked into the restroom. It was empty. He looked into the mirror over the sink and said, "You've shit your pants you idiot."

CHAPTER 2

A PARTICULAR JOURNEY

———◆———

IT HAD BEEN A FEW hours since the pants incident, and Wyatt stopped to get more gas. Maggie went inside. Wyatt took the moment of solace as an opportunity to look at Covington on the map and plan the trip to visit Uncle Luke. Wyatt figured that since Cora had called Charlie, she had likewise called Luke. There was a phone number included with the address Cora had given him. He sent him a text.

> "Uncle Luke, We may be in your area this week. Are you still in Covington?
>
> —Wyatt"

Maggie came out of the gas station with a sack of chips and crackers. She looked snidely at Wyatt as she got into the pickup. "A welcome alternative to pickled eggs and pork skins," Wyatt thought. Wyatt took his turn to go inside the small convenience shop. He headed to the restroom. He was finishing his business when he got a response back from Uncle Luke: "Yep, still here."

When they got back on the road, Wyatt was contemplative. "Let's camp in the mountains for a couple of days," he said.

"Where?"

"I don't know. Let's find a good place."

Once they had driven a while more, they approached a highway that read Mountain Parkway. A sign below denoted a scenic route. "Let's head that way," Wyatt said. Maggie gave no complaint. After a while of driving, they came to a sign for a park with campgrounds that looked interesting. Wyatt drove into the decorative entrance and went along the small scenic road, following signs to the campground.

Wyatt saw a fairly pleasant campsite near the shower house, which pleased Maggie. He pulled alongside and backed into the spot. The two got out of the truck. Wyatt unloaded the tent and began setting it up. Maggie got the food basket and sorted through and arranged its contents. Lastly, they built a small fire. Maggie lifted one of the Dr. Peppers from the basket and opened it. They sat there together quietly for a while.

Maggie soon needed some activity though. Wyatt was content to continue sitting. Maggie stood and went to retrieve the stamp binders from the pickup. She set them on the concrete picnic table. She opened the first one again and examined the puzzle more closely.

Wyatt sat peacefully as he reflected back on the events of the day, specifically his image in the mirror after the humiliating bowel accident. He glanced at Maggie, who was lost in the stamps. He thought of how kind and tolerant Maggie usually was. Now that had some time had passed since his embarrassment, he found humor in Maggie's vulnerability laugh attacks after slapstick accidents. As he looked at her, he still thought her plain, and wished she would fix herself up. He wished she was more motivated to do so. Then he thought, "She's been riding in a truck with a man who just shit his pants. Why would she fix up?" He sighed. After a while they became sleepy and went into the tent. They lay still in the sticky fall air, but both were content. They went to sleep.

The next morning they awoke. Maggie got up first. She began milling about the truck and tent. She opened the Dr. Pepper and ate a few chips. This woke Wyatt. When the weather was unpleasant, they stayed in the back of the truck, but they preferred the roomier tent when it could be set up. Both the back of the truck and the tent were lacking in padding, compared to the comforts of a real mattress, and contributed to their usual morning soreness. Wyatt got out of the tent and stood. He staggered over to the truck, moving his body around to usher out the soreness.

He reeled in shock at his reflection in the windshield. He thought he looked like a full-on bum. He turned and looked over at Maggie. She looked no better.

"When are we going to Uncle Luke's?" Maggie asked.

"In a few days, maybe. I sent him a message yesterday to say we would be in the area," said Wyatt.

"Did he reply?"

"He said he was still in Covington."

"Did you say anything after that?"

"No."

"Why not?"

"I don't want to rush it and seem weird."

"Weird? The whole thing is weird! People driving all over, sleeping in trucks? Planning to show up at a random uncle's house unannounced and trying not to be awkward?"

Wyatt knew she was right. In truth, he didn't necessarily know which way they were going or when. He needed a plan and felt like he was searching for one, though nothing he could think of was interesting enough to motivate him. "Let's hang around here for a couple days. Maybe we will fish some. It's pretty here," he said.

Maggie put up no resistance thus giving Wyatt a silent approval.

He spent the first part of the day tidying up the pickup and snacking. Later he took a brief hike and walked down to a nearby creek. He skipped a few stones and looked around for fish. He discovered how far across the creek he could piss. He walked back. This was Wyatt's idea of a pleasant morning. Maggie spent the morning drinking Dr. Pepper and fooling with the stamp collection. She saw that the glue had adhered each stamp to its neighbor, and the whole thing was now an unsolvable puzzle of random stamps. The mountings needed to be arranged but the pieces were all glued into a solid mass. After using a trial of spit, Maggie discovered that the glue was water-soluble. By midmorning, out of boredom, she was rigging up a coffee pot and a folded paper plate to collect steam. Slowly she steamed the stamps apart.

"They can be steamed apart, but it's going to be a pain… in…the…ass," she said across the way. After her announcement, she began to put the stamps and steam contraption away. She got two packs of crackers and split them into what they called lunch. Each had enjoyed the morning, but realized they would be ready to move from that place the next day.

Wyatt said, "You know, there is that park with the mammoth skulls near Covington. Let's stay there a couple days before we see Uncle Luke."

"Sounds good," said Maggie. They spent the rest of the evening strolling about the park. At sundown, they had nothing else to do, so they lay down in the tent. "It's early," Maggie said with a laugh. A few minutes later they were asleep.

The next morning they were up with the sun. Both were cheerful but felt physically rougher than they had the morning before. The ground under the tent was hard and unforgiving. Maggie began loading sleeping bags and moved achingly as she carried them to the pickup. Wyatt began disassembling the tent. He moved his sore joints and muscles slowly.

"I kind of feel like walking a while to work out some of this soreness, but I also want to load up and go," he said.

"Let's rock on," Maggie said after thinking for a moment.

Wyatt nodded. He continued to fold the tent and load it. He swung his arms and bent at the knees and waist to loosen his body. They were having a pleasant time, but some of the expected moments of misery were beginning to set in. They were both achy and both smelled stale.

They finished loading the truck and got in. Wyatt turned on the motor and sat still. Maggie began adjusting herself to get comfortable. Wyatt again noticed how dreadfully unkempt she looked. However, he smiled when he realized she hadn't complained a bit and was pleasant company. Wyatt wanted their lives to be better. He continued gathering his thoughts in the running truck. He held the steering wheel in both hands and tried to stretch out more of the soreness. Maggie tried to find something on the radio without success.

Wyatt relaxed his posture and looked out the window at the small campsite they were leaving. He thought of the many types of people who must have slept in this spot before him. "All types of people come here," he thought. He thought of rich men and poor men alike who might have been there. This made him feel somewhat kindred to these people he had never met. He mused how he might be like and different from them. Thinking of rich men being like him made him feel like a rich man, and at that moment he was. Here he sat in his truck after camping with his girlfriend. Inwardly, he felt like a prince, but outwardly he looked like a bum.

"What if you read that *Don Quixote* book to us?" Wyatt said. He thought it was a grand idea.

"I can't read in a car. I'll puke!"

Not to be deterred, Wyatt said, "Take my phone and see if you can find something like a book on tape to listen to." Maggie had no objections and began searching on his phone. She had nothing else to search in mind when the request came so what she searched for was *Don Quixote*. She found a free audiobook of *Don Quixote*.

"Here's *Don Quixote* for free," she said.

"Really?"

"Yep."

"That sounds good, hit it."

Maggie cued up the book, and it began to play as Wyatt drove the truck. Covington was north of them. If they followed the main roads, it would not take them long to reach the fossil park he remembered, however, Wyatt thought it would be fun instead, to drift north along the back roads. This would prolong their trip through a scenic area.

As Wyatt drove Maggie sat blissfully listening to the preface of *Don Quixote*. Neither really knew much about the story and did not know what to expect. Wyatt was nearly discouraged by the preface. The voice coming through was proper and to Wyatt seemed pretentious. He was quickly left behind by the reader's comments about translations. He heard a few names he did not recognize and a few places and dates that meant nothing to him. It frustrated him, though he did not say so. His aggravation was caused by the way intelligent people communicated with each other, and it was a language he did not understand.

He was somewhat relieved when the preface ended, and the real story of poor Alonso Quixote began. Maggie was enjoying it. The reader's voice made her feel as if she were in the company of aristocrats. With the voice in her ear, she straightened her posture as she and Wyatt drove north through small towns and communities. Maggie held the hard copy of the book they had gotten from Uncle Charlie. She looked at some of the illustrations that pertained to the section being read.

They had been driving for a couple of hours, and after a while, they pulled off the road. They were nearing their destination. They were hungry and found a pull-off overlooking a large field. Maggie paused *Don Quixote* as they got out of the truck to stretch their legs. Still having the intonation of the reader's voice in their heads, they continued speaking chivalrously to one another as they shared a drink from the gallon plastic jug.

"Our hour of our arrival approaches, brave Maggie," said Wyatt as Quixote.

"Aye, brave knight. Your enemies shall be befuddled with awe," said Maggie sarcastically. Wyatt pretended to be aloofly insulted. Maggie chuckled.

"We'll be there soon," said Wyatt. "We will listen to 'Old Don' until we get there."

"It's funny," said Maggie. They loaded back into the pickup and continued the journey. *Don Quixote* resumed.

After a while Wyatt saw a sign ahead that said "Big Bone Lick State Park." "There it is," said Wyatt. "Big Bone Lick!"

"That's the name of it?"

"Yeah, I couldn't remember the name, but that's it," Wyatt said as he smiled.

"How could you forget a name like that? Why in the world is it called that?"

"I think it is because of what the campers do there."

"What?"

Wyatt turned toward her and made the phallus-poking-the-cheek gesture with his tongue and right arm. Maggie looked even more confused, and Wyatt gave her an even more devilish smirk.

"Shut up," said Maggie. "Why is it really called that?"

Wyatt continued driving.

They soon came to the park, and in they went. They chose an empty camping space and backed in.

"This is pretty," Maggie said.

"Sure is."

"They should change the name of it."

The two of them got out of the truck and began setting up their typical small camp. They were both fatigued and sore from tent camping the past few nights. Their weariness brought shortness in their interactions with one another. After a camp of sorts was completed, they went on a short walk as the evening progressed. This improved their moods. They finished the walk and came back to the table of the campsite and sat down. Wyatt got up and fetched Uncle Charlie's *Don Quixote*.

"You want to hear some more?" asked Wyatt.

"Sure," said Maggie. Wyatt handed it to Maggie politely suggesting she read it. He was pleasantly surprised when she took it. He expected her shyness to extend into reading. Instead, she gave no objections and fumbled through the book until she came to where the reader had left off. She read aloud to Wyatt. He could not remember when he had heard her talk that long. She was talking articulately and with no bashfulness in front of Wyatt. They enjoyed the evening. Maggie's reading of the story helped them forget about the humid weather as well as the soreness they had collected. They addressed one another as "Old Don" would address Sancho. They chuckled when the horse, Rocinante, whose name Maggie struggled to pronounce, acted amorously toward some mares, only to be kicked and beaten for his effort. They laughed out loud about Quixote drinking and vomiting a potion given to him by an innkeeper. When Sancho did the same and it loosened his bowels, she had to put the book down due to laughter. After a moment, she wiped the sweat from her laughing face and said to Wyatt, "You and Sancho have something in common." She erupted with more laughter. Wyatt sat still with his lips pursed.

After a bit more reading, it was dark. Maggie had become tired, so they went into the tent. They went to sleep with no plans for the next day.

The next morning they got up and moved around in their usual way to work out stiffness. They had a few snacks that counted as breakfast. Sitting at the picnic table, Wyatt said, "Let's go see if Uncle Luke is at home."

"Do you think he will mind if we just show up?" she asked.

"I don't think he will care much either way," said Wyatt.

He did not know exactly where Uncle Luke lived. Armed with the address, Wyatt and Maggie began settling the camp. They soon drove off in the pickup, leaving temporarily to find Uncle Luke.

Finding his house did not take long, and by midmorning they had arrived at the house that matched the address. Wyatt pulled into the driveway. Before getting out of the pickup, he sat there for a second to see if someone would come to the door. Wyatt walked slowly toward the door and stepped back. Nothing. After a moment he did it again. This time he heard grumbling.

After a time an elderly gray-haired man looked through the glass at the top of the door. "I believe I'm good for now, but I appreciate it," the old man said, thinking Wyatt was a homeless man selling newspapers.

"Uncle Luke, it's Wyatt Mashburn, your great-nephew."

The elderly man opened the door farther. Maggie saw him greet Wyatt, and she got out of the pickup and headed toward the door.

At ninety-eight, Luke was a fairly feeble old man, though he was known for being quite nimble for his age. His friends and family commented on how well he communicated on social media. They did not know his small social media presence was actually managed by his bored son, himself aged seventy. This son, Cleveland, did so at his father's behest. Luke did not see well enough to message on his own. He and Cleveland had sought to spark conversations with distant family members and thus were sending friendly messages to third cousins. Most of the messages were, "Hi, this is Luke, your third cousin. I'm ninety-eight." One of these had reached Wyatt a few months earlier. The senior duo enjoyed it immensely.

"Nice to hear from you," was Wyatt's reply.

"Visit if you are in the area sometime."

Wyatt had not replied.

Luke had been a high school chemistry teacher as a younger man and had retired at age seventy. This feat brought him some local and familial notoriety twenty-eight years prior. Luke now peered out his door at the two homeless-looking people who knew his name and were wishing to be entertained. He was old enough that he had to concentrate on one thing at a time so he did not fall, and his actions were slow and cautious.

"What did you say your name was?" asked Uncle Luke.

"Wyatt."

"It's nice to meet you."

Wyatt could tell he was looking at him with an air of question, knew his ragged appearance was boogering poor Uncle Luke. Wyatt wanted to come across as pleasant to Uncle Luke, and say something to become familiar.

Not knowing why nor having a plan to do so, he decided he would change the cadence of his voice to sound more genteel like Quixote's reader. "I'm your third cousin twice removed, apparently," he said as he smiled graciously at Luke. "I got a message from you some time back about being a distant cousin." He gestured to Maggie who had heard what was said and was now standing behind Wyatt. "This is Maggie. She has come with me. You two have never met. We have been camping," he said, hoping to explain their presentation.

Uncle Luke opened the door wide and said, "It's a pleasure. Please come in." They went in and walked into a small tidy kitchen while Uncle Luke closed the door back and locked it. "Shall we go in the other room and sit?" Luke asked. He stood up straight, getting his bearings.

"Sure," said Wyatt. The three of them walked into the room, with Uncle Luke slowly bringing up the rear. Wyatt and Maggie sat on a small two-person couch across the room from Uncle Luke, who chose his favorite chair, which squeaked and was covered in all manner of cushions.

Wyatt began speaking with the same augmented accent as before. This change was accompanied by careful grammar and full pronunciations. Maggie thought it mildly humorous and decided to participate. She began interjecting subtle agreement and expressions of interest while Wyatt and Luke were conversing. Wyatt noticed she was doing so with exaggerated articulation. He began telling Uncle Luke they had been on a camping trip and wanted to sight-see for a while and visit some distant relatives if they were nearby. Luke asked them where all they had been so far, and Wyatt told him. He told Luke about Uncle Charlie and the stamps. He told Uncle Luke about the great gluey mess the collection was in and how Maggie had made a steaming contraption that could separate the stamps. Maggie nodded and smiled.

"Well, I just kind of rigged it up," she said. "I think I can make it better with more to work with," she finished. Uncle Luke was pleased by this. He did not see well, so he found her charming.

"How nice," Uncle Luke said to Maggie. "That reminds me of an old journal of my great-great-grandfather's. The pages are all stuck together. I found out they used hide-glue ink, and it's stuck together. Now it's quite ancient and falls apart when you touch it. It has been in that condition for decades, and no one has felt like taking on the task. It would be quite a task, and the result would likely be unreadable and would have no value."

"How neat," Maggie said. "I would like to see it." Luke did not reply to the statement, realizing that to retrieve the journal to examine it would require getting up and moving it from its closeted location. They continued talking.

Before long Luke decided it was worth the trouble to look at the journal and said, "Well, I'll see if I can find it." He shifted in his chair. A moment later he stood and began to walk toward a shelf in the room where they were sitting. He stepped into the corner and pointed up to a top shelf, unable to tilt his head and neck far enough to see it well. "That old battered clock you see up there belonged to the same man," he said. "He was an interesting fellow, apparently, and was a war hero in the War of 1812. I was told, he fought with Jackson in New Orleans. He had this old clock that didn't work. Some parts were even missing, but he wanted it with him at all times until he died. The family joked about the old clock being haunted."

"Who was it, Uncle Luke?" asked Wyatt.

"Barbee Collins," he replied.

"Am I related to him as well?"

Uncle Luke thought a moment and calculated, "Yes, I believe so. See if you can reach this old ticker, and take a look at it."

Wyatt stood and was able to gently remove the dusty instrument and set it on a small table. Its small top was rudimentary and used to feature hands and a pendulum, which sat atop a large, solid-wooden base. Wyatt thought it looked like the decayed junk you see in unsold piles in antique stores.

Uncle Luke moved closer toward a closet and opened it cautiously. "Wyatt, will you reach and get that boot box up in the corner?" Wyatt stood and helped him. "Take it over to that table," Luke said after Wyatt had taken it down. "Take it over there, and we will open it." Wyatt set it down and dusted the box with his hands and lifted the top gently.

Now gesturing to Maggie, Luke said, "Under those old newspapers is an old leather-bound book type thing, but you can't get anything opened or loosened because it's all stuck together, you see."

Since the episode with the steam—contraption was reported to Luke, it was understood that Maggie was the most experienced among them in dealing with stuck-together relics. Luke was designating Maggie to lift back some of the protective leaves of old newspapers, which she did. It revealed a fibrous-looking mass. Maggie placed it back after seeing this.

"Man alive!" she said. "It would be tough to get all that stuff apart without it falling to pieces."

"You wouldn't be able to read it once you did," said Uncle Luke. "What do you do with old things like this?" Uncle Luke asked, smiling at Maggie. "Why don't you take it with you? I have to find something to do with it."

"I don't know, Uncle Luke. That's a pretty old thing; you might should keep it," said Wyatt. Luke paused and looked at his distant nephew.

"No, you take it," he said. Wyatt said nothing else about it.

After this, they sat back on the chairs. Uncle Luke, now exerted, sighed and displayed his proneness to early exhaustion. "Are you two going to camp tonight?" Luke asked.

"Yes, sir," Wyatt replied. "We have a pleasant setup and are enjoying it."

"When will you head home?"

"Probably in a few more days," Wyatt replied, without really knowing.

Luke's response was only a tired sigh.

"You take a nap about this time?"

Luke chuckled. "Sure do. Do you?"

"Sometimes." Wyatt smiled.

"We should take one."

Wyatt smiled and shrugged.

"No, I don't have to, but lately I have been," Luke said.

"No, we will get out of your hair. We just wanted to visit and not impose," said Wyatt.

"Not at all, I enjoy the company," Luke said as he stood on his feet again.

Maggie and Wyatt realized he was gesturing to open the door for them. He really did want his nap.

Wyatt continued exchanging pleasantries as they gathered the boot box and old clock to take with them. While Maggie and Luke chatted, Wyatt made two trips to carry the items to the covered pickup. When finished, Wyatt walked back to the door to shake hands with Luke.

"Good luck to you two," Luke said. "I bet you will be glad to get home and get cleaned up."

Wyatt nodded affirmatively but was embarrassed about his disheveled appearance to which Luke was referring.

"For sure," Wyatt said.

Luke then reached out his hand to give Wyatt a rolled-up twenty-dollar bill.

"What's this for?" asked Wyatt.

"Some gas money for your trip."

"No, I can't take that. You keep it," replied Wyatt as he stepped out of reach from Uncle Luke.

Luke, now frowning, turned toward Maggie and said, "Take it for your trip."

Maggie took the twenty, thinking it rude not to do so. She put it in her pocket, hugged Uncle Luke, and thanked him. She and Wyatt walked toward the truck and got in. They waved at Uncle Luke, and he waved back before going back inside and closing the door to resume his nap plans.

After he closed the door, Maggie chuckled as Wyatt started the motor. "That was different," said Maggie.

"Yes, it was. Old men are crazy."

"I don't think we can stop and visit any more of your relatives. As soon as we sit down, they start giving us their old junk and run us off."

"Old men will give you half of their worldly possessions just to get you gone for nap time."

"And what is it about your family's relics getting stuck together?"

"We are tacky, I guess," Luke said.

The two drove back to their campsite. In the midafternoon, they walked and looked at fossilized behemoth bones. Evening arrived they sat on their concrete picnic table and finished off any food items left while Maggie continued to read *Don Quixote* aloud.

The evening was brisk but pleasant. Wyatt was still and listening to Maggie read. He thought about where they would go next. He thought about what he should do if they were to go home. He was also thinking about Maggie. What should he do about her? Their relationship was odd and new. They had been a couple for only a few months. Wyatt felt their relationship developing and hoped it continued to be enjoyable. She was frequently helpful and usually cheerful, but because she had known him as a friend before they were a couple, she knew him well enough to laugh as his funny misfortunes.

Wyatt looked at Maggie as she read. The dimming light helped her look prettier. The voice she used to read *Quixote* was different than her usual one, but it fit her. The changed voice made her sound more interesting to Wyatt. It made him stare at her more. As it does all men, *Quixote* enlivened

Wyatt with a regal spirit, and at that moment he felt like a bold knight. Maggie read a few minutes more, but growing tired she sat the book down. In her new enchanting voice, she spoke to Wyatt.

"I do believe I shall sleep, kind sir."

"A tent, my lady," Wyatt said, mimicking her style. The two stood holding hands and walked into the tent.

CHAPTER 3

WYATT MASHBURN

———◆———

WYATT'S EARLIEST MEMORIES WERE OF his parents, brother, and sister when they were young. He remembers his father, quiet and stoic, sitting at the small table in the school bus in which they lived. Wyatt had no memories of playmates or relatives. His memory of when his father and older brother died is more vivid. He also recalled the day the rest of the family was taken to live with his grandmother, whom he did not know at the time.

Wyatt's father, Louis, was a tall and handsome man who spoke slowly and with a constant air of certainty and finality. He was a man leery of the people around him. He felt that most Americans had forsaken God and reason, adopting lives that were artificial and toxic. He felt that schools were flawed, that they pushed an agenda of worldliness and false idolatry, and that they valued greed and lust over living a pure existence. As a result, his children did not attend school. Instead, he did it himself at the wooden table in their bus home. This wooden table in the bus was the center of the life Wyatt remembered. He remembered sitting at the table with his brother, Barton, while the father spoke to them. His father was funny and enjoyed making them laugh when he delivered the lessons. Their older sister, Cora, was also sometimes at the table. Louis taught them history and collected books for them to read. He taught them math as far as he could, and the children were generally good at it. Louis also gave them his running commentary on "other people" and how they lived and the foolish things they did. He taught them the tenets of subsistence farming and self-sustaining living of a brand familiar only to himself. These were things he felt lucky to have discovered and thought it his duty to pass along to his children.

Louis's father, Ralph, was born while the conflicts of World War II were raging across an ocean. He had grown up hearing men discuss battles they had been in and the heathen cultures they had encountered. He enjoyed complaining and grumbling and was known as being stubborn to the end. When the Korean War broke out, he decided he should enlist, as many young men his age did. Ralph was trained as a truck mechanic and spent most of his time in Korea mired in frozen mud and learning of man's ineffectiveness in war. He left the army in 1955 with a diminished opinion of mankind and its governments. He met Justine soon after leaving the army. She was a shy girl who didn't say much. Her aspirations were simple and being a comfortable house wife was success. She did not mind his grumbling as she mostly misunderstood it and was able to ignore it. Ralph got a factory job and a house, both of which he was very proud of. They were proof in his mind that he had "made it." In 1957 Ralph and Justine married, and two years later, Louis was born.

Louis was an only child and was eight years old when his father died. It was a simple case of pneumonia that went untreated due to Ralph's stubbornness. When he finally agreed to take medicine, it was too late. Louis's mother, Justine, was a simple woman who lived a typical sheltered housewife's life. She had relied on Ralph for most decisions and had not minded it. In fact, she had loved him for it. When Ralph died, she was directionless and would remain so for the rest of her life. Louis at eight was suddenly without an outside light. He could no longer inquire of the world. When Louis had questions, he had been able to ask his father.

"Dad, what is war?"

"Well, son, it is when politicians can't solve their problems without having to throw the lives of their neighbors into the fray." Louis would be left to ponder these types of answers as all children do when they obtain startling perspectives from their fathers.

"Daddy, what is pneumonia?"

"It is when you get a cough and the doctors try to hurry and kill you off with pills."

Justine, on the other hand, had no insights to offer her son now that Ralph was gone, no matter how inaccurate.

"Momma, what is an interest rate?"

"I don't know, son. Don't worry yourself with things like that." Justine loved her son, and saw to his every need, except conversation and exposure to the world.

Louis had to find his own answers. His mother now lived as a modest widow receiving her food stamps and commodities. She prioritized the feeding and hygiene of Louis, and he was well cared for, but unfortunately, she had no other knowledge of the world to share with her son. As a young boy, he studied the makeup and function of his surrounding world with the conclusions forming solidly in his mind, regardless of their reality. He had learned to distrust information and the importance of finding answers for oneself. Louis loved to read, and had a thirst for knowledge of how things work and why people do the things they do. He felt the events of his life had allowed him to seek and understand knowledge others were blind to. He found the world in constant error, and grew skeptical of the government, thinking all politicians to be untrustworthy. Banks were the nests of thieves. The few bits of life lessons told to him by his father let him know that hospitals were torture chambers, and doctors gave medicines to poison a person just to get their money.

When Louis was seventeen, he met a group of hippie farmers from Summertown, Tennessee, and admired their ability to escape the poisonous lives of their fellow countrymen. After a few months, Louis left his home near Huntsville, Alabama, and signed on to work as a farmhand on a commune near Summertown. There he was introduced to a community of people living alternative lives. He discovered there were others skeptical of the world. He observed humans living happily and at peace outside the prison of time clocks and factory-made food. Being a likable boy and coming from a pitiful situation, he was taken in by the gaggle of hippie farmers and given inclusion he had not known before. He stayed on the farm for three years and became one of them.

One of the families had a daughter named Marcy. She was plain and not inquisitive but kind and agreeable. She was prone to excessive anxiety but did not express much emotion. Her selections for a mate were limited in their remote part of the world but it did not matter after she met Louis. She saw that he was cautious and shrewd yet soft spoken. Her want in life was to find a husband to follow, and there was Louis. She fell in love with Louis and they were married after his second year at the farm. They lived in a small shack on the edge of a field of row crops. To Louis it was a blissful escape in which he felt uncontrolled by the world he feared outside. Marcy knew no better. Louis was her protector and provider and she was happy.

Marcy's family was fairly devout in their version of Christianity. The other families at the farm he knew were not religious really, but Marcy's family was. They were well supplied in New Testament translations and commentaries. Louis devoured these books, and they devoured him. The books became his obsession. In his mind things became clearer. To him the world was on a perilous path because it had forsaken God's will and had allowed Satan's vices to rule it. Louis developed this understanding more and deduced that the entire world was under Satan's rule—and maybe he was the only one who realized it.

One day a van load of odd looking people arrived at the vegetable auction the farm co-op attended. Louis was intrigued by them. He approached a young man about his age and began a conversation.

"Hey there, my name is Louis."

"Hi, I'm Josiah."

"I noticed your people coming in the van. Did you travel far?"

"Sure did, all the way from Nebraska."

Louis observed that all the males had on the same clothes. He noticed the cut and color to be particular and ubiquitous among them.

"Nebraska! That's a long way," Louis said.

"Yes, we are Prairieleuts. My father is here on business."

"What are 'prairie loots'?" asked Louis.

"Have you ever heard of the Hutterites?"

"No."

"Well, the Hutterites are kind of like Canadian Amish, except they live in barracks and wear funny bus-driver hats."

"Are you a Hutterite?"

"No, the Prairieleuts branched off from them many years ago and live in small communities in Nebraska."

"What do y'all do there?"

"Farm. Same as you."

"Do y'all go to school?"

"Yes, our mom does it every day for all of us."

"What does your farm look like?"

"It is really big but flat. It is really quiet as well. Just us out there on the prairie."

"Is it far from town?" Louis asked.

"Yep, about fifty miles. We hardly ever go. My parents want to avoid the town. My father doesn't trust the people there."

"Have you always been Prairieleuts?"

"Yes, I have, but my father's parents were Baptists, and he ran away. I've never met them."

"How did your parents become Prairieleuts?"

"Hmm, I don't know."

"They just joined?"

"I guess so," said Josiah.

"How do you join?"

"I don't think you do, really. You just become one."

"What do you mean?"

"I guess you move out to the prairie and call yourself a Prairieleut."

"How many other Prairieleuts are there?" Louis asked.

"I don't know. Not many. I met two other families once, but they were weird. My father doesn't like to associate with them."

The Prairieleuts soon loaded up in their van and were off. Louis continued to think about the odd life Josiah had described.

That night he and Marcy were close to falling asleep in the small shack. A sticky humid breeze dampened their faces.

"Marcy maybe we should move off and start our own place."

"You think so? Who with?"

"Just us," he said.

"What would we do?"

"Farm, like we do now."

"By ourselves?"

"Sure. We could do it. Lots of folks do."

"I guess so."

"We will probably have some kids too."

Marcy smiled and would agree to anything her mate suggested. She trusted him and did not want to face questions of this nature.

"It would be good for kids to be raised that way. Free from the poison the world will try to force on them."

Marcy had no response.

That fall Louis had saved up enough money to cheaply purchase a ten-acre plot on the edge of civilization, seventy-five miles from Summertown. The place had neither electricity nor telephone available—if they had desired to have it. That was a detriment to other buyers but a selling point to Louis. After the purchase, Louis found an old school bus at a salvage yard, and for an unbelievable deal, he had it hauled out to the property. Louis removed the axles and underpinned the space between it and the ground. He also installed a woodstove where the motor once was, and a chimney protruded outside. To everyone else, the whole spectacle appeared to be a vagrant's lair, but to Louis it was a shelter from an evil world.

The children did come. First came a daughter named Cora. She was born in the bus home, and Louis delivered her and performed the necessary tasks he had seen midwives do in Summertown. Two years later came a son named Barton, and three years later came Wyatt. He remembered seeing his sister helping her mother sew and cook. The days were usually busy with the chores and group labor that comes to a family living on their own. The farm work was sweaty and steady but not necessarily miserable. Louis tried not to make the work overly hard for his sons. "Work smart, not hard," he would frequently say to them. Louis wanted the lives of his children to be rich and pleasant but separated and not oppressed by forced labor. Louis made sure they had play time.

He remembered playing with Barton in the woods and creeks that were near the family's property. Fishing and throwing rocks at snakes in the creek were typical free-time activities. He could recall Barton and himself carrying a twelve-foot hardwood dowel they used to pry up rocks and pester turtles. It also served as a pole vault across the deep parts of the creek when they did not want to get their legs wet. One memorable episode from this time of his childhood involved an angry mother cow in a neighbor's pasture. She did not like the discovering young duo carrying a long stick in such close proximity to her calf, and thus gave chase. Wyatt remembered them vaulting across the creek just in time to escape the cow but laughing the whole way.

Wyatt also remembered evenings inside the bus. They liked to play chess and rummy. Wyatt couldn't remember a time, however, when he had left the small farm. None of the children had ever seen a town, but they had heard much about them. They read many books, but they were mostly classics, encyclopedias, and Bible studies. They had few real experiences to compare to what they read. Louis enjoyed delivering his version of the cosmos to his children at the small wooden table in the bus—there on the very spot where his children were born. It was next to the bunks mounted on the wall of the bus where his children slept. In Louis's mind, this was the best education possible.

These years ran together in Wyatt's mind as there was little difference from one to the next. However, the year they built the large brush pile did stand out in his memories. Louis and his two sons collected firewood throughout the summer and piled up the brush and debris into a large pile to be burned. The poison ivy had been especially bad that year, and both Louis and Barton had been smitten twice with the blistering itch. Wyatt had been a little more cautious being smaller than Barton, and managed to avoid contact. Louis decided enough was enough, and he and Barton were going to strip every sprig of poison ivy on the place and put it on the burn pile. They did this in ragged clothes that were thrown on the pile as well after the task was done. This even was followed by vigorously washing with soap and water.

That night Louis took his family to the brush pile and set it ablaze. He and Barton danced around the smoke and pushed it with their breath, one last insult to the pile of burning poison ivy that had tormented them twice before. Wyatt had seen the itching blisters his father and brother had suffered and wanted no part of it. Wyatt still remembered the laughing and the moments of happiness the firelight in the dark brought to the small family living on the fringe.

Cora was now seventeen and was a bit sharper than her mother, and she soon took command over most of the domestic oversight of the family. Barton was fourteen, and Wyatt was now twelve. The night of playing around the fire had kept them up late, and the family slept later than usual. Barton's cough woke them. Cora got up to get him some water. This awoke Louis.

"I've got it too," said Louis, coughing. He smiled, thinking it just from being in the smoke the night before.

Unfortunately, the coughs worsened, and both Barton and Louis were sore from coughing. No one in the bus slept.

The next morning they were all miserable but no one more so than Louis and Barton. Their whole bodies itched and ached. Their coughing was now producing blood-tinged sputum.

"I guess it's that dang poison ivy getting one last time," Louis said. He tried to smile.

"You think that's what it is?" asked Cora.

"Yes, probably. We shouldn't have been playing in that smoke."

"What should we do?" she asked.

"It will pass," said Louis.

"What would a doctor do?"

"Poison us, probably," he said. He laughed but was instantly choked and stifled by the unrelenting cough. That night Louis became feverish, and the next day, he was too weak to stand.

"Daddy, do you think we should do something? You are really sick, and Barton is getting a fever now," Cora asked, crying.

"No, girl, it will pass. Our bodies are strong. We will fight it."

The next day, Louis could not speak. Cora and her mother knelt beside him. They cried. They watched him breathe. Each breath was labored and colored with gurgles. They were still staring at him when he took his last furtive gasp and turned motionless and cold. Their weeping turned to screams and sobs. Cora ran outside, wailing and sobbing, and fell with her face in the dirt. Marcy lay childlike on the floor of the bus. She was on her side with her arms around her legs, sobbing. Each of Marcy's breaths was a wail. Wyatt sat frozen at the wooden table. No words could escape his mouth—only tears from his eyes.

"Momma!" Cora yelled. "We should have done something. He is dead! He didn't fight it! He is dead! My God! Momma, we should have done something!"

Marcy only sobbed more.

"Barton is going to die. He won't fight it! We have to do something!" screamed Cora, her face was a swollen mess. Snot bubbled at her nose, and drool came from her mouth as she screamed to her mother. No answer came—only sobs.

"I have to go get help! Barton will die like Daddy! I'm going, Momma!"

Marcy said nothing. Cora ran out of the bus toward the road. Wyatt remembered the sound of Cora's bewailing as she ran down the road for help until she was gone. The only noise in the bus now was Marcy's sobbing and Barton's gurgling.

An hour later a sheriff's car pulled up with Cora in the back. They got out and ran inside.

"My God!" said the deputy.

Cora collapsed and continued crying.

"An ambulance is on its way. Just hang on right here." The deputy went back outside to report this scene on the radio. Wyatt heard the deputy's words.

"One-two-five to county."

"Go ahead one-two-five," said a voice on the radio.

"The girl running on County Five that said her father died? She is from the ones that live in the old bus. The whole family is in there. The father has died, apparently, and another kid is sick and gurgling when he breathes. He does not look too good. EMT is en route."

"You say the father is dead, one-two-five?"

"That is correct."

"We will send county for him," announced the voice on the radio.

"One-two-five, this is Sheriff Goodnight," said a new voice. "Who else is in the party?"

"The other daughter. The mother is laid out on the floor and is crying. The older boy is sick in the bed, and a younger brother is sitting at a table, scared out of his wits."

"One-two-five, secure the location. Support is en route."

The ambulance arrived fifteen minutes later. The lights and sirens numbed Wyatt's already horrified senses. Two men from inside the vehicle got out and ran into the bus. Seeing Barton, they went back to the ambulance and got a stretcher. When they carried him out, Cora went with them. She cried convulsively as she climbed in and knelt next to her dying brother. One of the medics stayed in the back with them and was beginning to insert a needle with a tube on its end into Barton's arm. The other man closed the rear door and got into the cab driving off with the lights and sirens blaring.

Wyatt continued to sit motionless. The quiet had returned. Marcy was not sobbing any longer but was still lying on the floor. The deputy stepped back outside. A few minutes later a van arrived that said Wayne County on the side. Two men got out and spoke with the deputy, who then walked inside the bus.

"Ma'am? Can you come with me and let these fellas move Mr. Mashburn?"

Sobs and screams were her answer.

"Ma'am, please!" You don't have to leave yet. I just need you to get up and come outside with me for a minute or two."

Marcy wailed again and put her arms around Louis's body.

"Ma'am, please!" The deputy moved slowly forward and touched Marcy's arm. She bellowed and pulled away from the deputy and squeezed Louis tighter.

"Ma'am, please!" The deputy, now trying to lift her, continued his attempts to calm her. She continued to scream as he carried her out of the bus and lay her in the grass outside the door. "Just hang right here for a second, ma'am."

Wyatt had followed the deputy and his mother out of the bus and now sat in the grass next to her. He squatted beside them as the coroner's assistants went inside.

"What is your name?" The deputy said to the small, crying boy whose eyes were wide open and tear-filled but who had not yet uttered a word. Wyatt said nothing.

"Hey, fella, it's okay. I'm going to help you. What is your name?"

"Wyatt."

"Wyatt, I'm really sorry this is happening to you."

"Daddy died."

"Yes, I'm afraid so."

"Barton died."

"No, but he is really sick. They've taken him to the hospital."

"Is Cora there?"

"Yes." Then he turned to Marcy and said, "Mrs. Mashburn, I'm going to take you to Barton and Cora. Will you go with me? Wyatt will go with us. We need to go now. Will you come with me?"

Marcy stood. He led Wyatt and Marcy to the cruiser and helped them in.

When they arrived at the hospital, the deputy helped Marcy out of the car. He held her arm as he walked her inside to the desk and asked for the room of Barton Mashburn.

"He is in ICU-3."

The deputy took Marcy's hand again and said to Wyatt, "Okay, let's go."

Wyatt followed him down long, bright halls. There were beeps and alarms that were alien to Wyatt. When they got to ICU-3, it was a large glass room that was covered on the inside with blue curtains. The curtain in front of the door was pulled back. There lay Barton, with Cora sitting in one of two chairs beside him. She rested her head on his legs. The room was peaceful and quiet. Cora looked up when she heard the deputy approach with Marcy and Wyatt.

"He died, Momma," said Cora.

Marcy stood silent and raised her trembling hands as she leaned toward Barton. She moved silently and sat in the chair next to Cora.

"He quit breathing in the ambulance." Cora began to cry but still spoke words. "They tried to make him breathe with a bag, but his heart stopped. When we got here, they worked on him some more, but they quit after a while."

Marcy lay her head on Barton's chest, Her body beginning to tremble and then shake.

"He didn't fight it off, Momma. He died."

Marcy made a sound that Wyatt had not heard before. She screeched a low moan and kept screaming. This cry of unfathomable sorrow came from deep within her, and she screamed the entire breath from her lungs until no more could come out. She wanted to push the life from her body and never breathe again. To her sorrow, however, a new breath eventually came. With the next breath, she moaned and grieved as hard as she had with the previous one.

Wyatt began to cry. The deputy next to him again squatted to address him.

"My God!" said the deputy. "My God, son. I'm so sorry." He began to weep. "I'm so sorry this has happened to you." The deputy could speak no more. He stood and walked away.

The remaining Mashburns stood weeping. None of them knew what to do next. None of them wanted to do anything. They were paralyzed in a strange place by a horrible event.

A soft-spoken woman approached the three of them. Since Marcy and Cora still had their gaze on Barton, only Wyatt saw her appear.

"Hello, my name is Jennifer," the woman said.

Wyatt nodded.

"Is Barton your brother?"

"Yes," said Wyatt.

Cora heard this and looked toward the stranger. She stood and addressed her.

"Hello, Jennifer. I'm his sister," said Cora.

"I'm with social services. I'm here to help you through this."

"What do we need to do?" asked Cora.

"You don't have to do anything yet."

"What will happen to Barton?" Cora began crying. "What about Daddy?"

"I'll help you contact your family to make arrangements."

"We don't have any family."

"You all lived alone?"

"Yes."

"Will you be able to go back there?"

"No, we won't go back there," said Cora

"Does your mother have family?"

"No, they've moved off. We don't know them."

"Does your father have any family?"

"He was an only child, and his father died when he was a boy."

"What about his mother?"

"She lives in Alabama, I think."

"What about her? May I contact her?"

"We've never met her."

"Why is that?"

"I don't know. My father didn't visit much."

"Could you stay with her?"

"No, I don't think so," said Cora

"Maybe we should just call her?"

"I don't know how to reach her."

"I'll help you," said Jennifer

Wyatt carried no lasting memory of the following days between the hospital and his grandmother's house in Layton, Alabama. Justine, now eighty-two, did not fully register what Jennifer was explaining over the phone at first. Jennifer had arranged for a van to take them after speaking with Justine on the phone. Jennifer explained to her that her son whom she had not seen in many years had died, and his family was left with no place to go. Justine made her explain it again but more slowly: her son's widow and two remaining children whom she had never met were coming to stay with her.

"Can they stay with you? Would that be okay?" asked Jennifer.

"I...I...guess so," said Justine.

She did not get the full picture until Wyatt, Cora, and Marcy got out of the van and introduced themselves.

Wyatt did not find living in his Grandmother Justine's house unpleasant. It was comfortable, and his bed on the couch was an upgrade from the bunk on the bus. His grandmother was not much of a conversationalist, but he was glad she was not a scolder. Talking about Louis and Barton was too sad for the family, so they avoided it, Wyatt included. But occasionally Wyatt would ask Justine what Louis was like when he was younger.

One day Cora gave Wyatt a butterscotch candy and Justine commented. "Wyatt, seeing you open that candy reminds me of Louis. He loved butterscotch," said Justine. Wyatt was intrigued by this and enjoyed the imaged of his father eating candy as a boy.

"Did Daddy eat a lot of candy when he was a kid?" asked Wyatt remembering that Louis used to tell him a Barton sweets would rot their teeth out."

Justine chuckled, "He did till his father told him it would rot his teeth out. He was always a worrier. His father Ralph was too." Justine's eyes began to tear so she said nothing more.

Cora and Marcy stayed together in Justine's spare bedroom. In the weeks to come, Cora learned to love her grandmother who returned the sentiment. She needed a helpful soul like Cora at this point in her life. Marcy was present only in body. She sat quietly on the couch most of the time. She frequently stared at the wall, saying nothing, with tears running down her face.

Wyatt was ten when they moved but was not allowed to far from the house or library. A few years later when he was thirteen, Cora would let him explore his surroundings more. Marcy did not impose any rules on Wyatt, it was Cora who finally allowed him into the small, urban world of Layton, Alabama. It was a small town north of Huntsville. No longer in the middle of a pasture in a bus surrounded by silence, his environs were now paved and filled with a city's sounds. Motors running and casual car honks in the distance were the sounds in the air. A new set of places was now within walking distance. There was a Walmart two miles away. He could walk to the grocery store in ten minutes. There were all manner of stores selling bright clothes and flashy shoes of all varieties. There was a comic book store, as well as a library complete with a kind lady inside who helped folks find anything under the sun to read.

As Wyatt explored this new domain, he did not have the same fears of it that his father had. The town was busy but neither frightening nor uninviting. Wyatt, like his father, would be left on his own to learn about the world, but Wyatt did not find it vile. He spent the next three years in this existence, soaking it up like a sponge. He learned to communicate with other people, and things he needed on his own.

There was little to no money, so to improvise and discover alternatives was the norm. When the county came by with papers, Cora marked the box "home schooled," so he did not need current trends, nor did he know of the things other children his age squabbled over.

Cora, now grown, got a job at the grocery store. It was in walking distance from Justine's house. It was here that she soon met an awkward boy named Lawrence. She spent more and more time with him. Wyatt, on the other hand, spent his days at the library. Like his father he craved knowledge of how the world worked. Louis read books to discover what he should fear and hide from. However, when Wyatt read, it made him want to seek out those places and experience them in person.

When Wyatt was sixteen, he got a job at the nearby comic book store. His awkward appearance limited his employment options at most places but not so much at Layton Comics. The other employees were as odd as he was. One of the employees was Sol, and he had large, circular piercings in his ears and told hilarious jokes. The other and most senior employee was Mikey. Mikey was in his thirties and had intricate tattoos and spoke of aliens. He was friendly in a love-and-peace sort of way and thought Wyatt was a cool kid. Wyatt learned banter and skillful sarcasm from these colorful characters. They showed Wyatt all sorts of things to amaze him. They also showed him dirty magazines that embarrassed him. They played all types of music as well. Mikey let Wyatt drive his car around the parking lot, and he even took him to get his learner's permit.

Wyatt did well at saving the money he made. Having never been exposed to it, he did not really know what to spend money on. He decided he was going to get a car. After a few months at the comic book store, his savings were growing. While walking home, he saw a green Chevy truck sitting in a driveway by the road—for sale. Wyatt instantly saw himself driving the highways and sleeping in the back, going anywhere he pleased. He approached the truck and walked around it. It was a bit rusty in places, and the tires didn't match. The odometer said 180,000 miles. Wyatt made his way to the house as the end of the gravel drive and knocked. A white-haired, grumbling, black man came to the door.

"Yeah," said the man.

"Hello, sir. I like your truck."

"Humph. Thirty-five hundred."

"Does it run?"

"Yep. Runs."

"Anything wrong with it?"

"Nope. Runs good. Thirty-five hundred, like I said." The man began to close the door.

"I'll have it in two weeks."

"Eh. It will probably be gone by then."

"Wait. Can you hold it for me?"

"Nope. Thirty-five hundred gets it."

"I'll be back in two weeks." The man closed the door. Wyatt could think about nothing but the truck. He knew some lucky soul with cash in pocket would buy it before he got the chance. A paycheck would come in two weeks that would put his holdings at $3,500, but until then he had to wait. That night he told Cora his plan.

"I don't see why you can't buy it," said Cora.

"I can in two weeks. I think I'm going to get it. I can go anywhere."

"Where would you go?"

"Everywhere."

"You don't have a license."

"Mikey will take me. I can use his car for the test."

"There will be taxes."

"Taxes? What do you mean?"

"After you buy it, you have to register the truck in your name at the courthouse, and they charge a fee. I heard Lawrence talking about it."

"How much will it be?"

"I don't know," she said.

"Guess!"

"Lawrence said he paid four hundred, but his truck cost ten thousand. I bet yours will be around one-fifty or so."

"I won't have that in two weeks."

"You'll just have to save a little longer."

"No, it won't be there! The man will sell it. It could be gone in two weeks as it is."

"What are you going to do?"

"I don't know." He sat silently for a moment. "Could you give it to me?"

"Me?" said Cora.

"Yes. Would you loan me the money?"

"I don't know, Wyatt. I was saving it."

"I'll pay you back."

"You won't be able to. You will have gas, and don't forget about insurance. You have to buy insurance as well. Did you think of that?"

"Yes, Mikey told me about the insurance, but I can pay it monthly with my checks. I'll give you rides!"

This got her attention. "Where would you take me?"

"Anywhere you wanted. Please, Cora! Will you give it to me?"

She began to cry. "Wyatt, you will leave."

"Leave? What?"

"If I give it to you, I know you'll leave, and I won't see you anymore."

"No, Cora. I won't."

"Yes, you will. You will be gone. There is no reason for any of us to stay here if we could leave. If you get that truck, I will not see you again."

No, Cora, I will still be here." As soon as he said these words, he knew they were not true. He would not stay.

"Now, Cora, don't cry. You will still have Lawrence."

"Huh. Lawrence," she remarked.

"Why do you say that? You love Lawrence. Y'all will probably get married soon, won't you?"

"Yes, probably, but I still don't want you to go."

"I'll be here."

A tear rolled down her cheek as she declared, "I'll give you the money."

"Thank you, Cora. I'll still be here."

The next day Wyatt walked to the comic book store. His shift started at noon and he stayed until 8:00 p.m. That day when he opened the stickered door, Mikey was standing against the back wall, organizing and sorting the colorful action-hero comics. Wyatt walked around a display of collectible baseball cards and stood behind the cashier's counter.

"Mikey," he said.

"Yo!" said Mikey.

"I need your car again."

"I don't know. It's going to cost you this time."

"I need to get my license."

"Right on! You gonna pass the test?"

"Yes, I've been reading the booklet."

"Cool, I'll take you tomorrow," Mikey said.

"Thanks, man!"

Right on, dude. You gonna get some wheels?"

"Yeah. You know that green truck for sale on Martin Street?"

"Dude, I saw that one. That is Chet Taylor's old truck. He's had it forever. Be warned though; he is a grouchy old sumbitch. His brother George used to sell killer weed, but unfortunately he got arrested."

"I wonder if his truck is any good," asked Wyatt.

"Hell, I bet it is. Chet kept it shiny. That Chevy was his pussy magnet."

"Uh! Yuck!" said Wyatt.

"Hell, it might become your pussy magnet."

"I doubt it," Wyatt said.

"What are you going to do when you are driving around in Chet's old truck and a bunch of pussy jumps out and attacks you?"

"I've heard it's best to play dead when animals attack."

Mikey howled. He liked Wyatt's quick wit. Mikey continued, "The problem is that when pussy attacks, something happens in your brain, and you start attacking it back."

"You are so full of wisdom, Mikey."

"Just glad to pass it on, little bro. Just passing it on."

"Thanks, man. If I ever get waylaid in a pussy attack, I'll call you first for help."

Mikey's lips exploded with spit and laughter. "Right on! Call me! I'll come running!"

The next day Mikey took him to the driver-testing center. Wyatt handed them his birth certificate and learner's permit that he knew they would ask for. He passed the paper test with ease and in Mikey's car performed with confidence and calm the maneuvers the instructor requested. Within an hour a lady in a blue uniform called his name. At the counter, she returned his birth certificate and presented him with a driver's license. Once the task was completed, Mikey took Wyatt back to Justine's.

When the two weeks were up, he took the money to Old Chet, who signed the line of the title and gave Wyatt the keys.

"Is that it?" Wyatt asked after Chet handed him the title.

"Yep." Chet closed the door.

Wyatt started the truck and blew out the white, puffy, burnt-oil smoke that settles in old motors. He drove it to the courthouse and paid the fees as Cora had predicted. They handed him the title, and he departed. As Wyatt walked to the green pickup, this time, he realized it was truly his. He looked at the title with his name on it. He looked at his driver's license. It was his ticket to anywhere. His world was now different.

He continued working at the comic book store for a few more months, still stowing away his money. He learned more about the seamy side of life from Mikey and Sol. He took Cora on occasional trips she requested or errands she needed, keeping his promise. A bulldozer came and took out the old school-bus home they had known in the past, and an agent from the county arranged for the property to be auctioned off. Marcy received the check, but she had no inclination to do much and was fine with staying quietly in Justine's home. Justine, feeble, was glad to have quiet company.

One evening Wyatt was sitting on the small, pebbly, concrete porch when Cora came out to join him.

"What are you thinking about?" she asked him.

"Nothing, really," said Wyatt. "What are you thinking about?"

"Nothing." She sat next to Wyatt and stared at the sky over the scant yard.

"Well, I guess I have been thinking," she confessed.

"What is it?"

"Lawrence has a grandmother up in Illinois that will give him a place to build a house. He wants to get married and go up there. I've decided I'm going to go with him."

"When are you leaving?"

"Oh, it will be nearly next year, I'm sure."

"That doesn't sound too bad. Do you think you will be happy?'

"Yes," she said. "Have you thought about what you are going to do, Wyatt?"

"I don't know. I've considered getting a camper top for the truck and heading out on a road trip."

"Where would you go?"

"No idea yet. Maybe west. Or maybe east, I don't know. Probably both, eventually."

"How long will you be gone?"

"I don't know yet. What if I find someplace and it is really nice, and I get a job and stay there for a while before moving on?"

"That sounds fun. Will you send me postcards?"

"Sure."

It was a few months later when he did leave. He saved until he came across the aluminum camper shell he was looking for. Wyatt explained to Cora and Marcy he was going on a short trip for a few days and not to worry about him. His sister begged him to be careful and to be sure and send postcards. He agreed, saying he would be back soon.

He headed west. He drove through Athens and Florence and into Collierville before coming to Memphis. As he drove past the humongous buildings, Wyatt grew curious about the activity within them. The giant face of Muhammad Ali on one of them smiled as he headed across the giant green bridge that took him over the Mississippi. Once across, he wanted to see it again. He found a turnoff to a green patch of grass and a park that sat along the river in view of the bridge and sky-scrapers. He backed into a spot where he could lie in the back of his pickup and see the river, and stayed there his first night.

As Wyatt sat on the tailgate of his pickup looking at the river, he felt reborn. He felt like a citizen of the Earth. He had no place that he called his native home. The world was his home, and he wanted to see more of it. His day was turning to dusk. He was tired but couldn't sleep. In the distance he could see a boy and two girls who looked to be in their twenties taking off their clothes to skinny-dip in the Big Muddy. They did not notice the green truck in the distance. Wyatt saw a glimpse of one of the girl's bare breasts and turned away. Laying down under the metal camper top, he tried not to think about them and stared into the darkness. He thought of all the places he could go; the hard part was choosing just one of them. He couldn't decide yet and was gleeful that he did not have to do so. He would just start driving as he did today and find another nice place where he could stay there for a bit. Now Wyatt was doing what he wanted to. Soon he found sleep on his modest foam mattress, sleeping bag, and pillow.

CHAPTER 4

CITIZEN OF THE EARTH

———◆———

IT WAS THE END OF May when he left Layton and awoke next to the Mississippi River. It was the chirp of birds and the briskness of the morning that woke him. He got out of his truck and snuck to the edge of the site to pee. He closed the camper shell and hopped into the cab. It was warm from the sun. He sat there waking and feeling the sun warm his face through the glass. After a moment he started the engine and pulled back onto the highway. Heading west, Wyatt watched the buildings and bridges of Memphis disappear behind him.

The interstate moved fast, and he liked it. The world felt small now that places he wanted to explore were only a few hours away. He thought also that being in the cab of his pickup was comfortable. He turned the radio to the stations available as the chosen one would fade in and out on the FM radio dial. The AM dial stations stayed longer and were usually folks with city voices talking about things he didn't understand. He did not know much of what they ranted or raved about, but the topics interested him.

He drove on I-40 west and got to Little Rock, and he saw the gray hue that floats above the city when you approach it. He approached a sign for the roads to Dallas–Fort Worth or Fort Smith. He decided to go south to Texas, but he did not know why. Perhaps to him it sounded more exotic and adventurous. He met the same decision that took him to Shreveport when he came to Texarkana. After passing through Shreveport and finishing a second tank of gas, he was ready for a change of scenery and a change of pace from the interstate. South of Shreveport he took an exit to get gas in Mansfield. From there he traveled west, passing through Nacogdoches. He soon came to signs announcing the Davy Crockett National Forest. The green of the foliage lay below an umbrella of the approaching blue night sky, turned orange by the clear evening sun. The sliding daylight made Wyatt's fatigue and sleepiness known. He was driving through the beautiful greenery when he passed over a bridge, and under it he saw an inviting clearing, accessible by a side road. He took the road and parked along the bank of the river until night fell. Soon, Wyatt was asleep in the back of his pickup.

His slumber was broken by a loud knock on the window of his camper and a light shining onto his face and sleeping bag. Wyatt sat up, startled.

"Hey, there," said a man's voice. "This is the National Park Service. This is a no-camping area."

"Oh, sorry. I didn't realize. I'll move. Very sorry," said Wyatt.

"Yeah. Thank you," said the ranger as Wyatt climbed out of the back.

"Where are you from, fella?" asked the ranger.

"Layton, Alabama."

"You just passing through?"

"Yes, sir. I just pulled over to catch some sleep."

"Unfortunately, you will have to stay in an allotted camping area, and they are currently full."

"Oh, I'm really sorry."

"Do your people know where you are?"

"Yes, sir. I left three days ago. I'm just doing some camping." Wyatt was now awake and sitting in the cab of his pickup. The ranger checked his identification and confirmed all was in order.

"Well, be careful," said the ranger.

"Thank you," Wyatt replied and drove away.

It was nearly midnight, and the startle of being wakened by an authority figure kept him alert now. He drove west in the dark. The lights of Waco and Abilene had come and passed by morning. Dawn came as he passed Midland, and he got back onto the interstate. By noon, he was approaching El Paso.

The numbing effect of a night without sleep yielded a surreal feeling for Wyatt as he looked out to see the brown, rocky earth the new day's light had revealed. How different it was from the dark-green and lush country of his youth. Perhaps it was due to being awakened by chastisement, but Wyatt did not want to stop driving. He needed sleep, but he felt it was safer to keep moving. The road through El Paso turned north and the signs to the mountains of Albuquerque seemed like the right way to go. By the evening, he had reached Albuquerque and continued north. When he neared Santa Fe, he saw signs for camping in Carson National Forest and knew sleep was unavoidable. As daylight fell away, he found a small campground next to a rolling mountain stream. He put the required handful of dollars into the campground fee-deposit receptacle and lay down in the back of his pickup. The night was long but peaceful, and he slept with no interruption.

The next day he slept late into the day. He walked around to stretch his legs after getting up. He was captivated by the incredible beauty of the place. The water in the stream was cold, but he could see skittish fish moving in the deeper parts. The barks of the trees were curly, and the stones on the ground and in the stream were round. The trees were thick and green but with needles—not like the broad leaves of the east. The beauty impressed him, and he thought it a paradise. He stayed in this spot for two days.

The days were good for him and affirmed the success of his traveling mission. He decided to resume driving north along the small roads through the Rockies. These roads took Wyatt through high mountains and across low valleys, with breathtaking views in between them. The night of this first day back on the road found him near Grand Lake in the Northern Rockies. There he found another streamside campground that had the same remote charm as the one he had found the day before.

The place was so beautiful he contemplated never leaving. He did not imagine the mountains to be as majestic and inviting as they had been. He wondered if this would continue as he went north. After a couple nights of camping, he continued north, and the sights overwhelmed his expectations. He came to Loveland and continued north through Cheyenne, Wyoming. There the earth changed from green to amber but was equally as beautiful. He caught some sleep at a truck stop just south of Sheridan.

He was listening to the AM radio as he came into Billings. A crop report came, on telling about cattle and hay prices. Wyatt thought it interesting. Soon he heard the voice on the radio make an announcement that caught his attention.

"Roguers are still needed in Hill County. Wheat farmers have asked the ag extension office to announce the need for temporary help over the next two to three weeks. Good wages with room and board are available. Anyone interested should please report to the Hill County Agricultural Extension Office."

Wyatt was not sure what roguing was but didn't think it could be too bad. Wheat farming sounded interesting, and the cash he had brought was dwindling. Two days later he found himself walking into the extension office to inquire about roguing in Hill County, Montana.

"Can I help you?" A gentleman approached him.

"Yes, I'm Wyatt Mashburn, and I heard an ad on the radio that roguers were needed."

"Ah-ha. I see. Have you rogued before?"

"No. Is it hard?"

The man smiled and shook his head no. "No, it's mostly pulling weeds."

"Oh, I see."

"Yep, Japanese sage grass. A certain percentage of foundation wheat seeds planted have unwanted Japanese sage seeds mixed in. This sage grass will put out seeds and get into the fall wheat harvest. So those rogue sage-grass stalks have to be pulled up. The sage grass is taller than the wheat for a while and can be seen at eye level across the wheat fields. One just has to just walk about and sight in and then pull up rogue sage grass."

"Oh," said Wyatt. "I believe I could do that."

"Yes, I'd say you probably could. Where are you from, young fella?"

"I'm from Layton, Alabama."

"Do you have family there?"

"Yes, a mother and a sister."

"Do they know you are here?"

"Yes, sir."

"Are you in any trouble?"

"Why, no, sir. I'm just driving around for the summer."

"Well, I'll tell you. I know of a family that has a boy about your age, and I was talking to them the other day, and they were looking for an extra roguer. Let me call them."

"Thank you," said Wyatt.

The extension agent sat down at his desk and thumbed through an old Rolodex until he found the number he wanted. He dialed it.

"Jan, this is Phil Leder at the extension office. Is Tom available?" A brief pause. "Tom, Phil Leder here. A young fella from Alabama came in today and said he was looking for some roguing. I thought of you since he is about Tommy Jr.'s age. Well, it's hard to say, but he seems like a good kid... Sure, I'll tell him. Sure, any time."

The agent smiled and turned to Wyatt. "That was Tom McIntyre. He and his wife and son live about thirty miles from here and are good people. They are hardworking and a little shy. I don't mind helping them, and I hope you'll do a good job for them. Mr. McIntyre wants to meet you, so I would head there now."

"Thank you very much." This was happening fast, but Wyatt was eager. Phil gave him the address on a sheet of paper along with a map showing to get to the McIntyre's. He was there in an hour.

When he pulled into the driveway he noticed "McIntyre" on the mailbox. The house was a modest tan-brick house in the middle of ten thousand acres of wheat. There were two huge barns that dwarfed the house. They covered a few tractors and an aging combine. When he pulled up to the house, a man and his son walked out to meet him. The man looked to be in his early fifties and was balding with a slight belly paunch. His glasses were thick and repaired with tape. "Are you Wyatt?" he asked.

"Yes, sir. Are you Mr. McIntyre?"

"Yes. Welcome, Wyatt. Phil at the Ag office said you might could help with the roguing. Have you done it before?

"No, sir. Is that a problem?"

"No, not really," said Mr. McIntyre. Tommy Jr., his son, who was seventeen did not say anything while his father was speaking, but smiled and nodded to Wyatt. "You will be helping Tommy mostly. You'll pick it up. Where are you from?"

"Layton, Alabama."

"What brings you to Havre, Montana?"

"I was just driving, and I heard an ad on the radio."

"Driving? From Alabama to Montana? What for?"

"No reason. Just looking around."

"For what?"

"Nothing, really. Just looking," said Wyatt.

"Does your family know you are here?"

"Yes, of course." Wyatt had become aware now of the point of this line of questioning.

"We just don't want any trouble."

"Oh, no, sir. I won't give you any."

"Thank you, Wyatt. We hope it works out. You can stay in the barn apartment next to the combine. It's not bad. Plus you'll get twelve dollars an hour while you are working."

"Thank you, that sounds good," said Wyatt.

"You can stay as long as you are not a troublemaker." Tom smiled at Wyatt after he said this.

"Oh, yes, sir. I won't give you any. If ever you are not happy, just say, and I'll be gone without a word."

"Thanks, Wyatt. I'm sure it won't come to that." Tom turned to his son. "Tommy, take Wyatt to the barn and show him where to stay. You can look at the fields before supper and get a good day's start tomorrow."

Tommy walked toward Wyatt. He had the same awkward bearing as his father but was kind and curious about Wyatt.

"Hi, I'm Tommy," he said.

"Hello," said Wyatt.

"It's this way. Come on, I'll show you." Wyatt followed him to the big barn and Tommy showed him the small room with a dresser and bed that was to be his home for a few weeks.

"Are you from a farm?" asked Tommy.

"No, not really," said Wyatt. "I lived on a farm when I was a kid, but my father died, and we moved to Layton."

"How come you are in Havre?"

"I'm not sure. I've been driving for a little over a week. I heard on the radio they needed roguers."

"You never rogued before?"

"No. Do people like it?"

"Some do. It gets boring just walking though fields pulling weeds, but it is not hard. I'll show you. It's probably what we will do all day tomorrow."

Wyatt did not have any belongings to put into his new living quarters, so Tommy showed him more of the place. The wheat fields were beautiful moving like the sea in the gentle wind. After a while Tom Sr. came to where Tommy and Wyatt were.

"Wyatt, did Tommy show you around?"

"Yes, sir. Thank you. It's a beautiful place."

Mr. McIntyre was pleased with Wyatt's manners. "My wife, Jan, is inside. She is making some supper," said Mr. McIntyre. "She would be out here to meet you but she said it would burn if she left it." Wyatt smiled. Mr. McIntyre was also trying to make Wyatt feel welcome. "Tommy, get cleaned up, I'm hungry. Wyatt, you join us. We will discuss tomorrow's roguing," he said.

"Sure. Thank you," said Wyatt as his stomach growled with hunger.

Soon Wyatt found himself eating a warm home-cooked meal with the odd McIntyres. Jan and Tom Sr. were friendly and welcomed Wyatt. Tom Sr. gave Wyatt and Tommy more instructions for the coming day, speaking with calm authority. Tommy took what he said and nodded with little comment.

"Why don't you boys plan to make the most of the day?" said Mr. McIntyre. "It would be good to start by seven and take a lunch." Tommy appeared to dislike the suggestion but made no dissenting comments.

"Yes, sir," said Tommy, while Wyatt nodded in agreement.

After supper was over, Mr. McIntyre suggested both boys go to bed early in order to be well rested. Wyatt welcomed the idea.

The next morning at 6:30 a.m. sharp, Wyatt was awake when Tommy showed up next to the barn in an old truck. Jan made sausage and biscuits for them and sent them with Tommy in a large lunch bag. She hoped this would keep them fueled for the day. Jan was a kind woman and felt it important to be helpful. She reminded Wyatt of his sister Cora in that she stayed busy, and contributed her thoughts.

Tommy drove them to the spot his father had suggested. The fellas got out their feed sacks that would hold the pulled weeds. Tommy squatted down at eye level to the green stalks to show Wyatt how the sprigs of Japanese sage grass poked up above the rest of the wheat. At this vantage point, the otherwise unseen rogue weeds were visible. The sprigs fifty or so yards away were the first to go. Tommy walked out, pulled them up by the roots, and put them into his sack, trying not to spill any seeds.

"That's how you do it," said Tommy.

"Got it," said Wyatt.

The work was not hard, and the scenery was beautiful. Since the job was new, Wyatt did not find it boring. He enjoyed it. He also wanted to make a favorable impression on the McIntyres. He worked intentionally fast. At the end of the day, Wyatt was tired and so was Tommy. Their truck was now loaded with full sacks. Tommy drove them to the burn pile where the seeds would be destroyed. Mr. McIntyre saw the amount of sage grass the two had pulled, and he was pleased with their effort. He invited Wyatt to supper again. This time Wyatt sat at the table even more hungry than the previous evening. He now had a day's labor behind him. This work had helped this generous family who was now happy to feed him.

"What did you think of roguing today, Wyatt?" asked Mr. McIntyre.

"It was fun," he said with a smile.

"Sure it was. Well, you did pretty good on your first day. How do you feel?"

"I'm a little sore in the legs and back, but it is not too bad."

Mr. McIntyre noticed Wyatt's raw hands. "You have to watch your hands as well. Those weeds will blister you after you pull a few hundred of them. Be sure to wear those soft roping gloves in the barn. You'll be miserable after a few days if you don't."

"Thank you," said Wyatt.

After supper he decided to just go to bed and be rested for the next day, which he expected to be similar to this one. And like the day before, Tommy came at dawn and picked him up, and they drove to another large, square field. Wyatt put in another hard day for the McIntyres. That night at the supper table, he earned more praise from Tom Sr.

"Well, Wyatt, you seem to be hanging in there," said Mr. McIntyre.

"Yes, sir. Thank you," said Wyatt.

"You and Tommy are moving kind of slow this evening."

"Yes, sir. I'm a little sore, but I'm okay."

"Tommy, hold off on that big section by the creek until the day after tomorrow. I don't want y'all getting lame or blistered."

"What do you want us to do instead?" asked Tommy.

"Why don't y'all take the four-wheeler down the center line to the creek? Pull any rogues you find in the ditch. Take the rifle, and try to plink any gophers you see in the lower field. I've been seeing them along the edge."

"Okay," said Tommy.

Wyatt noticed Tommy's countenance lift as plans for the next day turned from the drudgery of roguing into riding on a four-wheeler and shooting gophers.

The next morning began like the previous two, except that Tommy came to pick up Wyatt with an old Honda four-wheeler instead of the pickup. On the front of the four-wheeler was a rifle rack, and in its prongs was a seventeen-millimeter rifle with a mounted scope the size of a quart soup can. Tommy called the rifle "the seventeen." Wyatt rode behind Tommy as they whizzed down the center roads between the fields. They stopped occasionally to pull some sage grass. The weeds also made their way to the ditches that lined the roads between the fields. The fine yellow glacial silt making up the road sprayed from the tread of the four-wheeler's tires as Tommy hugged the corners and curves. The wind blew their hair, and both of them were smiling like bandits when Tommy came to the edge of the field inhabited by the gophers. Tommy pointed to the gopher mounds in the distance. Wyatt barely made them out. Tommy got the seventeen out of the rack and set it on a tripod on the ground and gestured for Wyatt to watch. In the distance, Tommy pointed to a stick standing near the mounds, then looking through the scope, fired a shot that struck the base of the stick from three hundred yards away.

"You try, Wyatt," said Tommy.

Wyatt lay down next to the seventeen like Tommy had done. When he looked through the scope, he saw the crosshair on top of the extremely clear gopher mounds that were barely observable without the rifle's optics.

"If you watch and wait, you'll see their tan heads moving around the mound. Put the cross hairs on them, exhale, and pull the trigger slowly," said Tommy.

Just as Tommy had described, within moments there was a small tan head moving erratically around the mound. The head paused for a few seconds to look around and Wyatt placed the crosshairs. He exhaled and fired. The gopher's head disappeared and a red stain was left on the dirt behind where Wyatt was aiming.

"Did you get one?" asked Tommy.

"Yes."

"Well, wait a bit, and there will be another one."

A few minutes later, another tan gopher noggin was moving around the mounds. Wyatt took aimshot with deadly accuracy. This is how the boys spent the day, riding the four-wheeler around the dirt roads, stopping to dismount when they saw sage grass along the road or to set up the seventeen to plink gophers when mounds appeared.

"What do you think, Wyatt? This is pretty fun, huh?"

"Sure is," said Wyatt.

"You are a good shot," said Tommy.

"Thanks. It has been a long time."

"You used to go hunting a bunch?"

"No not really," said Wyatt, "but my dad liked to shoot rifles. Me and my brother used to have target shooting contests with him. He would joke and say we distracted him when we would get closer to the bullseye than him."

"Did you run away?" asked Tommy.

"No he died. And my brother too."

"Oh," said Tommy, shocked by this. "I'm sorry."

"It's okay."

"How did they die?"

"They got sick after inhaling poison ivy smoke in a brush pile," said Wyatt.

"Man I'm sorry. That must have been tough, how old were you?"

"Ten."

"What about your mom?"

"Well, me and her and my sister Cora, went to live with my grandmother, Justine, after that."

"Do they know you are in Montana?"

"Not yet, but my sister says she wants me to call her or send her a letter if I stay some place."

Tommy was intrigued by Wyatt's parental laxity but thought the circumstances depressing. He know more but was too embarrassed to ask further questions. "It's about time for supper," he said.

"Mmm, I'm hungry."

"Me too! Let's head back."

The two rode the four-wheeler down the road past the area they had covered previously. Tommy picked up speed to accentuate the excitement of the trip home. Tommy was rounding one of the corners that went around a smaller field. Wyatt saw a set of gopher mounds they could plink the next time they were assigned this task. Wyatt raised his arm to point it out to Tommy. He turned and saw the mounds in the distance and nodded. This slight distraction caused him to miscalculate the clearance of a gatepost and the front tire of the four-wheeler. When the right front tire struck the post, it rolled the four-wheeler, sending its riders over the left side and into the soft bank of dirt on the other side of the road. When Tommy lifted his head and dusted off his face to make sure Wyatt was okay, he noticed Wyatt was lying face down in the dirt. Tommy jumped up and ran toward him.

"Wyatt! Wyatt! Are you okay?"

Wyatt groaned and tried to roll over. Tommy helped him gently. He gasped when he saw Wyatt's face. Two of his teeth were bleeding and pointing in odd directions. His lip was bleeding along with the abrasions on his cheek. There was more blood now pouring down his face from a deep cut in his hairline. The blood was getting in Wyatt's eyes, but his wiping it away only smeared his face and hands with blood.

"Oh God, Wyatt! You're hurt!"

Wyatt groaned as he felt the rest of his face and ran his fingers over his mouth. He felt the protruding teeth, and groaned more when he realized his condition.

"Wait here," said Tommy. He ran over and turned the four-wheeler back onto its wheels. Wyatt heard the motor start. He ran back over to Wyatt. "Wyatt? Can you stand?"

Wyatt began to stand on his feet. Tommy helped him up slowly. Wyatt was able to stand, but the blood in his eyes hindered him from moving.

"Oh man! Your teeth look pretty bad, and your head is bleeding like shit! Oh man! I'm really sorry, Wyatt! Get on the four-wheeler, and I'll take you to the house! We had better hurry!"

Wyatt slowly got onto the four-wheeler. Tommy got on in front and finished the trip back to the house. When they got back to the house, Mr. McIntyre saw Tommy helping Wyatt off the four-wheeler. He then saw Wyatt's face.

"Holy hell, son! What happened?"

"We flipped the four-wheeler, and he hit his face on a rock in the ditch," said Tommy.

"For shit's sake, why weren't you being careful? This is pretty bad. Wyatt, are you okay?"

Wyatt moaned.

"Shit! You need a doctor!" Mr. McIntyre walked into the house. A few moments later, he came out with some towels and Mrs. McIntyre. She applied the towels to Wyatt's bleeding head and noticed his teeth.

"Good heavens Wyatt," said Jan. "We have to get you there now. Oh, you poor thing," she said.

Once she examined the injury further she decided it was serious. Assuming command of the situation, she took Wyatt by the arm walked him toward the car. "Tommy, go get me the stack of older towels from the closet. All of them!" She then looked at Mr. McIntyre. "Tom, the man will be here in an hour to fix the combine tire, he can't reschedule because it's too far out. He will only come this way once a week. You will have to stay here, and I will take him into Havre."

"You're right," said Tom Sr.

"Help me get him into the car," she said. Tommy was running back with the towels.

The family helped Wyatt into the back of their older Ford Taurus wagon. Jan got in to drive and headed down the road.

"Wyatt, are you hurting?" she asked as she accelerated.

"Uh-huh," Wyatt's replied.

About forty-five minutes later, they arrived at the small hospital emergency room. Wyatt got an X-ray and a series of staples in his scalp. His face was bandaged. He was also given a cup that contained his left upper canine tooth and the one that sat behind it. Wyatt could barely process this due to the pain he felt. Jan brought him back home and helped him onto the couch next to the kitchen. She spent the next two days tending to him.

By the evening of the second day, he was able to sit upright. He heard Tommy and Mr. McIntyre coming in for the day and gathering at the table. Wyatt stood to join them. His face was bruised, swollen, and scabbed. His mouth bulged with swelling and was purple. The skin around both of his eyes was black. The whole family tried to hide their cringing when he sat down at the table with them.

"You doing any better?" asked Tom Sr., trying to be polite.

"Yes," Wyatt was able to say.

"I'm really sorry," said Tommy. "Is it still hurting pretty badly?"

"Yes, but it's okay. It's not your fault," said Wyatt.

"I'm not so sure about that," said Tom Sr. Tommy looked at the floor. "Well, anyway. You just rest here until you are ready."

"I'll be ready tomorrow," said Wyatt.

"I don't know. That seems a little too soon," said Jan.

"I'll be careful," said Wyatt.

"Well, I admire the toughness, but you don't have to," said Tom Sr. "Just take it slow."

Wyatt nodded.

He was able to return to roguing the next day, though every step and movement was painful. Bending over to pull the sage grass was the worst. When he bent over the blood rushed into the swollen parts of his face and reignited the pain. This would improve over the coming days, and he would soon again be an efficient and agreeable hand for the McIntyres. He was moved into a spare room in the house, at Mrs. McIntyre's insistence.

After a few weeks, roguing was over, and the family was planning the harvest. Mr. McIntyre asked Wyatt to stay past his roguing conscription and help with the harvest. Wyatt agreed and stayed until fall.

The harvest came and went, and the wheat fields became silent as winter approached. The previous winter Tommy had gone to work in a cafeteria for three months at a ski resort. He asked Wyatt if he wanted to go with him. Wyatt did, so Tommy made a call, and they were hired.

They left in November for the Big Sky Ski Resort. Wyatt enjoyed his time there. The cafeteria on top of the ski mountain was an exciting place and was full of comradery like the comic book store had been. There were pretty girls from all parts of the world coming through. All manner of people and accents were there. Wyatt continued to save his money and lived modestly with Tommy. That winter was fun for Wyatt, and it passed quickly. When March came the seasonal help of the resort was thinning out and heading home. Tommy had another gig for them.

"My dad called," said Tommy.

"How is he?"

"Good. My uncle in Mississippi called him. He is planting of pumpkins to be sold by the truck load. He wondered if I could come help him with the planting for a couple of weeks before going back to help Dad with spring wheat. Dad told him about you, and he said he could use you. Do you want to go with me?"

"Sure, I guess so," said Wyatt. So the next week, the two of them headed south to Jericho, Mississippi, just north of Tupelo. There he met Tommy's uncle Geoff and aunt Wanda, the pumpkin farmers.

Geoff and Wanda McIntyre were an older couple whose kids were grown and had families of their own; they lived in town and were unavailable to help Geoff with his pumpkin project. Geoff planned to sell two truckloads of pumpkins at the annual auction in August. The time of planting was key to them being all harvested at the same time, and Geoff wanted them all planted in a week. In addition to the truckloads of pumpkins, Geoff had an additional side project that consumed his attention, and that was his giant pumpkins. Each morning and every evening, he walked out to the edge of the garden where the septic tank drainage from the house kept the ground wet and fertile. This location was Geoff's secret to growing the "big mamajamas." He would crawl around the plants and pumpkins looking for any signs of rot. The girth and rotundity of his belly prevented him from breathing fully, which turned his bald head red when he squatted down to check the plants. He hoped to win the honor of biggest pumpkin at the two local fairs in which he would enter specimens. He expected to win and had done so a few times in the past. The trophies from these accomplishments were place in the holiest of places on the mantle over the family fireplace.

The two weeks of planting came and went. Wyatt and Tommy had been a good help to his uncle. Geoff knew Tommy must return home to Havre, so he asked Wyatt if he would stay and help him until roguing season, when he could go back to Havre. Wyatt liked Geoff and Wanda, and they treated him well. Their banter was funny, and they had accepted Wyatt as family. Wanda was graceful and talkative, and enjoyed Wyatt's company. Wyatt knew their acceptance of him was partly out of pity when they found out about his youth, but it was also because that is the nature of rural folk. He decided to stay with them when Tommy left. Wyatt also thought that he might not go back to Havre. It might soon be time to move on.

Wyatt was a top hand through the spring and into the summer, helping tend the growing pumpkins and other chores that were needed. Geoff continued his daily monitoring and nursing of the future champion giant pumpkins. By July the pumpkins were getting closer, and the giant ones were behemoths. Geoff searched them all over for signs of softness or rot that would disqualify them from competition.

Wanda had prepared a Fourth of July meal of her famous pintos and cabbage. They emitted a pungent odor, but their taste was divine. That evening Wyatt sat at the table with the couple.

"Wanda is famous for these beans and cabbage," said Geoff.

"They sure are good," said Wyatt.

"Thank you," said Wanda.

"Be careful with them now, Wyatt," said Geoff.

"Why is that?"

"Her beans are famous for something else as well."

"Oh yeah? What is that?"

"Now, Geoff, be civil," said Wanda.

"Well, you will see tomorrow," Geoff said and laughed as he and Wyatt got another helping.

Geoff was right. The next day he and Wyatt were feeling it. All three of them woke with the vapors. The smell of sulfurous farts was filling the house now. The three of them took their turns in the bathroom, and afterward the smell in the house was so foul that Wyatt needed to go outside. Geoff soon came waddling out as well.

"Ooh whee!" Geoff said. Those beans have lit me up!"

"Me too," said Wyatt. Geoff let off another tremendous fart and moved away from his own smell in disgust. The two of them did their best to do the day's chores, but they were frequently interrupted by large billows of gas and sprints to the bathroom. It was so bad that the area of the garden where the giant pumpkins were planted in the effluence of the septic tank began to reek of sulfur. Their expulsions continued into the night.

The next morning the situation was resolving itself and activities were returning to normal. Wyatt was about when he saw Geoff looking at the weeds along the edge of the giant pumpkin patch. Geoff detected the normally green weed sprouts had yellowed. Wyatt walked out to him.

"What's up, Geoff?"

"Those beans must be extra potent. Look at how it's killing the weeds over the fill line." They both chuckled and walked away.

Wyatt was working on a fence before noon when he heard Geoff shouting, "Wanda! Damn it, Wanda!"

Wanda came running out of the house. "What is it? What is it?"

"Those damn beans, Wanda! Damn it! I knew it!"

"What are you talking about?" said Wanda.

Geoff pointed to a rapidly changing brown spot showing up on the bottom of his largest giant pumpkin. He was kneeling down and looking at it closely.

"Oh no," said Wanda as she knew this meant disqualification. Wyatt had walked up by then and was observing them.

"What is it?" asked Wyatt.

"A spot," said Wanda.

"Oh no!" said Wyatt.

Geoff, still kneeling next to the rotting giant, looked up at Wanda with a tear forming in his eye. "It was those damn beans, Wanda! Look how the plants are yellowed near the fill line!"

"Oh, Geoff, you know that spot must have been forming before that," said Wanda, trying not to laugh.

"No, it wasn't either! You know it was those beans! Those egg-bomb bastards have gaulded me and killed the one that was going to win. It was those beans! Why couldn't you have just made meatloaf?" Geoff then looked at the ground, unable to speak further. Wanda and Wyatt walked away, feeling terrible for Geoff and his disqualified giant, and they held their giggles until they were far enough away that Geoff couldn't hear them. It was a few days before he would return to his usual jovial self.

August came to the pumpkin farm. Wyatt had decided not to return to Havre for roguing duties. Geoff had been planning to take the smaller pumpkins to an auction but had met the owner of a petting zoo who wanted the whole load delivered to him. Geoff thought this a better deal for him and made plans for him and Wyatt to deliver them. The petting zoo was two hours away, outside of Springfield, Tennessee.

The following week, Wyatt and Geoff began to pick the bowling ball–sized orange orbs and pack them into boxes that would be loaded onto Geoff's large flatbed trailer. This took a couple of days, but they soon had them loaded.

"We will leave tomorrow morning with them," said Geoff. The next day came, and they hauled them to the petting zoo. When they arrived Geoff got out to speak with the head man. A couple of employees were sent over to help unload the large boxes. The boxes were to be stacked into a pumpkin pyramid near the main entrance of the petting zoo. It would take all day. One of the helpers the zoo had sent was an older man who worked quietly at a steady pace. The other was a tall, plain girl who was also a quick worker. The girl noticed Wyatt and smiled at him once but kept working. After a couple of hours, Wyatt paused to rest and spoke to her.

"What's your name?"

"Maggie," she said.

"Are you from here?"

"Yes."

"How long have you worked here?"

"A few months. It was supposed to be seasonal, but they asked me to stay on full time," she said.

"You like it here?"

"Sure, it's nice."

"You ever get tired of it?"

"No, there is usually something going on."

"Hmm. That does sound good."

"You should talk to Mr. Henry. They are needing some folks to stay through the winter."

Wyatt smiled with his lips closed in order hide his missing teeth. "Well, I might look into it."

Maggie smiled and worked on.

"Maggie, what is your last name?"

"Fields. Maggie Fields."

CHAPTER 5

MAGGIE FIELDS

———◆———

MAGGIE HAD GROWN UP IN the confines of her parents' limitations. She knew little of the world when she graduated high school, but was clever and good with her hands. She had also inherited an ability to get lost in a daily routine without needing much variety. Maggie's parents were simple people who lived in Springfield, Tennessee. Her father, Edward, was slow and did poorly in school. He was bashful and did not enjoy school. He soon decided it wasn't for him, and he found more satisfaction working at a local grocery store as a shelf stocker. It was peaceful work, and it suited him since he spoke slowly and was not handsome.

He did that line of work until he retired. He met Maggie's mother when she came into the grocery. He had been working there for a few years and knew most of the faces of the people who came in and out, though, he did not usually have a need to speak to them. Melinda Vantrese was twenty years old when she first came to Flanders's Grocery. She, like Edward, was a little slow.

Melinda's father was a machinist and was moved to Springfield by his company. He moved in to a small house on the edge of town and brought a crippled wife and an awkward daughter. Melinda was plain, pale, and pimply. She walked oddly while staring slack-jawed at the ground. She was able to walk to the store from her house. On the day she first saw Edward, she had been sent to the grocery to get some flat spaghetti. She came in and began looking through the small selection of pastas and saw only round spaghetti and not any flat. Edward was nearby, stacking cans of beans. Melinda walked over to ask him if Flanders's carried flat spaghetti. Edward told her they did not. That was their first encounter.

Four years of this went by. A few times a month, Edward might see Melinda. Rarely did she ask for assistance, but she usually came into the store, got her items, and left. Sometimes she would wave silently at Edward.

One summer a sandwich cart had been set up outside the grocery. Edward took a lunch break and went out to the sandwich cart as Melinda also arrived to get a sandwich. Edward smiled and nodded while he got his sandwich. Melinda did the same. A week went by, and the same event occurred. When Edward saw Melinda, he smiled and nodded to acknowledge the coincidence. She smiled back. After he paid for his sandwich, he turned to Melinda to avoid rudeness and said, "See you next week."

To which she replied, "Okay."

Edward had to think about what had happened for a couple of days. The week passed, and as predicted, Melinda appeared at the sandwich cart for lunch. But this time she waited until Edward came out. When he did, they walked together to the sandwich cart. That was their first date. This carried on for four or five weeks until it was announced that the sandwich cart was closing for the season. Melinda asked Edward if she could bring a hot lunch to the grocery break room for him once a week. He agreed. After two months, it turned into every other day. After two years of this, they were married. Edward continued at the grocery while Melinda cleaned church buildings in the evening. Ten years later, Maggie was surprised to find out she'd become pregnant. Maggie was born a few months later. Edward was forty, and Melinda was thirty-six.

Due to her parents' simple nature, Maggie was not exposed to many things outside of what was discussed at school or on the radio and television. She was not that into boys and did not pursue them. Her plainness and lack of fashion left her unpursued by them in return. She caused no problems in high school and received As and Bs. She did not enjoy school and assumed college would be worse. She also did not have the money for tuition, and she had not scored any scholarships. The advisors at school told her financial aid was an option for everyone, but the form was never completed. Her parents did not push her either way and she felt no social pressure to go. When she graduated from high school, she worked a few months in the grocery store where her father had been employed. She like her father was awkward but not slow. Working at the grocery allowed her to try a different social setting than school, where she avoided contact and faded into the shadows. Her bashfulness abated amid the cans of beans and she found herself joking with customers.

When she was old enough, she got her driver's license in hopes she would be free to travel, but she lacked the funds for a car. Her father, Edward, had an old pickup truck but it was rickety and probably would not have made it out of the county, and the seat was somewhat painful to sit in. She did run a few local errands for the grocery store manager in his Buick from time to time, and she liked it very much. Driving inspired her to be more adventurous, and made her long to see places farther away, like the Grand Canyon.

After her seventeeth birthday she saw a sign for seasonal employment at a petting zoo. She laughed at the idea at first, but later convinced herself it was worth looking into. Mostly out of curiosity, she rode the neighbor's ten-speed bike to the petting zoo. She guessed it to be seven miles away. She applied and got the job much to her surprise and it paid two dollars better than the grocery. She continued to borrow the neighbor's bike for two weeks but soon bought a slightly better bike at a pawn shop with her own cash. When an apartment opened up in a four-plex near the zoo, Maggie moved in. Some other employees of the zoos lived there in the neighboring units.

She first met Wyatt when he arrived with a truckload of pumpkins the zoo was going to sell as souvenirs to its visitors.

She and a couple of other were tasked with helping unload the pumpkins. Her first words to him were casual and inconsequential. He seemed interesting but rough looking. She thought he was friendly, and suggested he apply for work at the petting zoo after he asked her a few questions about working there. After they unloaded the pumpkins, he told her good-bye and that he hoped he would see her again in two days when he brought the second load.

Two days later when Wyatt and a reloaded pumpkin trailer returned, she helped unload them and spoke again with Wyatt. Before leaving, Wyatt conversed with the owner about a job that was posted for winter. Wyatt got the job and was happy to report to Maggie that he would be back in a week to sign on with the petting zoo for the winter.

When he came back, Maggie helped him find a vacant apartment next to hers. It was a peaceful place but small. He was glad Maggie was there to provide some company. In the spring when he agreed to stay on and work at the petting zoo through the summer, it was partly because of her. The apartments where they stayed were located in a single-story wooden house that was divided into four apartments. When the next spring came around, he signed on again.

By the time Maggie had her eighteenth birthday, Wyatt had had his nineteenth, and they were an odd couple. They soon decided they would save money by moving in together in a larger apartment when it came available while they continued at Henry's Petting Farm through the summer and fall.

As two years of working for the petting farm approached, Wyatt was looking for a change. He thought Maggie would probably go with him if he left. One day, they were in the Henry's Petting Farm truck, delivering a load of nanny goats to another farm in Flintville, Tennessee. They unloaded the happy goats and were heading back when they saw a small, older mobile home that wore a sign that said, "For Rent. $150 Monthly." They pulled into the driveway and looked at it. This might be the change of scenery he was looking for. Maggie liked it as well and had no major objections either.

When winter came to Henry's, Maggie and Wyatt did not stay on. Rather, they moved into the little trailer home in Flintville. Their cost of living was negligible and scraped by in ignorant bliss through the winter doing odd jobs and waiting for spring when they could find work. Spring came and Wyatt found work mowing yards but the urge to travel was distracting them. Wyatt got a free Android phone, with a one year contract from Verizon. He enjoyed exploring the digital map with satellite images of any place in the world. They had gone on a few short day trips through the winter in Wyatt's pickup, and had enjoyed them. This mutual enjoyment of seeing new things together was something they acknowledged without words and was the spark that changed their relationship. They were on one of these trips when Wyatt bought a half gallon of pickled eggs.

CHAPTER 6

A CLOUDY DAWN

———◆———

TWO TRAGEDY- AND CALAMITY-STEERED LIVES now sojourned together. To an observer, their situation was pitiful and their
appearance derelict. Wyatt and Maggie both had been situ-
ationally sheltered from the larger society as children. Their
prison's walls were unconventional in that the captives did not
know a difference existed outside of them. The escape from
their previous lives brought the freedom they expected but
also surprise at the abundance of lifestyles and experiences.

They had been met with acceptance and generosity in
their recent lives. They had learned that working hard and
proving honesty has great rewards. Since leaving their parents, they had learned of the lives of their relatives—people
who came from similar progenitors but went down vastly different paths. Wyatt contemplated this the evening they drove
back from Uncle Luke's while listening to *Don Quixote*. Wyatt
wanted the paths he chose to be good ones. He also wanted
any path he chose to be open.

That night Wyatt and Maggie slumbered in the back of the truck. Their sleeping bags were aged but neat. Birds of the night filled the damp air with noise. The hours of the night passed peacefully. A calm haze of fog clouded the dawn but not the regal spirit with which they had retired the night before.

Wyatt continued to lie still in the tent. Shortly Maggie rolled over and saw him awake.

"What are you thinking?" she asked as she began to stir.

"What do you think about heading back?"

"I guess that would be okay."

Wyatt exited the tent, and now good at it, took down the tent and loaded their things.

"Before we go I'm going to go to the shower house and hose off," said Wyatt. Maggie got two towels and a small bag of toiletries. They walked hand in hand to the bath house, each going into the "His" or the "Hers." Wyatt did his shower routine quickly and finished while Maggie was still going. He could hear her singing and saying occasional words to herself through the thin walls, and she could hear him.

Wyatt dried his hair and looked into a mirror. "What a damn mess," he said. Wyatt was disgusted as usual by the vagrant he saw in the mirror. "Maggie," he said, loud enough for her to hear him through the wall and running shower. "I'm getting a haircut today!"

A pause. "Oh okay," she said. Then another pause. She chimed in with a voice like Sancho or Quixote himself, "Then so shall I!"

They finished their toweling and put on their clothes. They met again outside the shower house and walked hand in hand back to the truck. They put their things away and drove.

They shortly came to a sign for a small hair establishment that read, "Family Cuts. Ten Dollars." Wyatt signaled and turned in. They got out and climbed two stairs. Maggie opened the door. Inside, a lady and her eighteen-year-old son greeted them.

She was the owner and was a soft-spoken and sweet soul who looked at Maggie and asked, "Can I help you, dear?"

"We would like haircuts," said Maggie.

"Well, sure," said the lady. "I can get you right now." The place had no other customers, and Wyatt sat down next to the son. He was a friendly fellow with a few tattoos, and he smelled of pomade and aftershave. "He is learning to cut hair," the lady said of her son. The son smiled at Wyatt and nodded politely.

"He's just learning," she said, "but he really does a good job. He doesn't have a barber's license yet, but if that is okay with you, he could cut it for seven dollars. A discount. Since he is just learning. He's real good."

"That sounds good to me," said Wyatt. He sat in the boy's chair. The boy began with the drape and tissue around the neck, being extra careful as he was being tried as a beginner. The boy did not want to mess up Wyatt's generosity.

"What would you like?" asked the boy.

"I don't really know," said Wyatt. He thought for a moment. "Something like the king would wear."

"Yes, sir!" The boy did not know what king he was talking about. The king of England? The king of rock 'n' roll? It didn't matter. A high fade with a part and pomade was coming.

Maggie had gotten into the lady's char. Standing behind Maggie, She smiled oddly at Maggie in the mirror, noticing the mess with which she was now presented. She asked Maggie, "Anything in particular?"

"No, not really," said Maggie. The lady proceeded without any further input from Maggie.

Maggie and Wyatt sat in their chairs silently. They stared at the mirrors as their coiffeurs did their work. In the corner of their eyes, they each caught glimpses of the other's progress, and they smiled at each other.

Wyatt's hair was finished first. The boy had indeed done a stellar job. Wyatt looked sharp, like a James Bond character. He liked it, and so did Maggie. He gave the boy his seven dollars and sat on a chair. The lady was still in the middle of Project Maggie. Out of sympathy, the lady said nothing of the extra Maggie's neglected hair was requiring. "Just shaping now," the lady said. Wyatt realized Maggie was getting way more than ten dollars' worth.

"What colors of makeup do you usually wear?" asked the lady.

Maggie hesitated. "I don't wear too much," she said.

The lady was not surprised. "You know, I learned a trick. I go to the fancy makeup counters at the mall and let the counter girls do up my face," the lady explained to Maggie.

"They tell you what all they used and then you go to the flea market and get it cheap. The girls will give you some samples also. You should stop by the mall on your way out of town, since you are getting fixed up today."

"Maybe," said Maggie.

Wyatt thought it was a good suggestion.

The lady finished with Maggie. Maggie looked into the mirror at her clean and straightened hair. It was neatly trimmed and curled under the edges. She liked it. She had undergone quite a transformation. She stood up and looked at her new do from different angles in the mirror. She thanked the lady and gave her the twenty that Uncle Luke had given her. The lady gave her a ten back. Maggie walked toward Wyatt and the door. She looked at Wyatt.

"You look slick," she said.

"You look pretty," said Wyatt. They both turned red and walked out the door, thanking the lady and her son once more.

"Good luck to you," the lady said. They got back into the pickup and headed toward home. Still fiddling with her hair, Maggie turned on *Don Quixote*. Wyatt was silent as he listened to the story and watched Maggie examining her hair in the rearview mirror she had turned towards her.

When a mall came into view, Wyatt made his way there. He pulled in to the large parking lot of one of the department stores. They got out and walked in. Maggie said, "I'm not buying anything. It's too expensive." They milled around the perfume counters, trying smells, while they scoped out the makeup counters. Over next to a shiny silver sign with lights was an unoccupied makeup lady and a chair. Maggie began to drift that way. She knew what to do. When she got to the counter, she smiled at the lady and began looking at her wares.

"Anything in particular you are looking for?" the lady asked Maggie.

"No, just looking for something different."

"I've got a couple of new things. Do you want to sit in the chair and try them?"

"Sure! I guess." Maggie got into the chair and the lady began looking at Maggie's face. The lady noticed that Maggie was wearing no makeup.

"It's always a good idea to not wear anything when you come in to try new things," she said. Maggie said nothing as the lady grabbed various brushes and began powdering. Wyatt stepped back and watched from a distance. Wyatt watched the lady apply various foundations and colors. Maggie was making mental note of the items and techniques the lady was using.

"Is this close to what you would normally use?" the lady asked.

"Yes, pretty close," replied Maggie. The lady worked a little while longer. She applied some fine lines around the eyebrows and tweezed a few hairs. Lastly she chose a lipstick and applied it. Then she penciled a similar color onto Maggie's lips.

"Well, that's about all I've got," said the lady. "What do you think?"

"That's fine. Thank you," Maggie said as she got off the stool.

"Did you want to get any of these today?" the girl asked Maggie.

"Yes, probably," said Maggie. "Let me look around a little more and think about it first."

"Sure thing, I've got some samples of what I used, and I'll put them in a bag for you. She did so, and Maggie thanked her. Maggie walked around a little more among the other counters, pretending to "think about it" as she had promised the lady. After an appropriate time, she walked toward Wyatt and they exited. Maggie looked one last time at her reflection as she walked outside. She liked what she saw. Wyatt liked it also. The woman who was getting into his pickup now looked much different than she had earlier that morning. They drove the rest of the way home, listening to *Don Quixote*.

The home to which they arrived was a rickety single-wide house trailer. When new it was a design feat of efficiency, but that was decades ago. Now it was small, dingy, and weathered. The rent was affordable, and the leaks were easy to fix. Wyatt and Maggie kept it fairly picked up, and it wasn't necessarily cluttered but was shabby in its entirety. As Wyatt and Maggie were arriving, they saw the familiar house but were not filled with the joy of homecoming. In truth they were happier on the road.

When they arrived and got out, Wyatt unlocked the door and checked that everything was as it should be. It was. He began unloading the pickup. Maggie went inside. The brown-orange carpet was familiar but not welcoming. Wyatt brought in the suitcase with the stamp collection and the box with the old journal and sat them on the kitchen table. He went back out and returned with the old clock and set it on the side table next to a sofa. He brought in the last few things from outside and closed the door.

There was not much to scrounge for eating in the house, but Maggie got what there was and began to prepare something to knock the edge off their hunger. Wyatt went into the bathroom. He finished his business and as usual looked into the mirror. This time he did not reel in shock. His look was improved. He liked his new haircut, and it made him feel refined. He smiled, but that made him frown. His missing teeth still revealed the look of indigence that Wyatt did not care for. He walked out of the restroom. Maggie was standing at the stove, facing away from him. Her hair looked nice. Her make-up looked nice. Wyatt found himself attracted to her. It made him happy.

Wyatt called Mr. MacAnally and told him he was back. Mr. MacAnally had some yards for Wyatt to mow, and he said he could start tomorrow.

"Maybe I should go and see if that market is hiring," said Maggie.

"Nah, just hold off." Wyatt said this, but he didn't know why. "Why don't you go into town tomorrow and get a couple of new things to wear at the Goodwill? We need something to go with our new hairdos." Maggie smiled and nodded. The two began eating the sparse vittles Maggie had prepared.

"What are you going to do this evening?" asked Maggie.

"Not much. Piddle around the house. You?"

"Nothing."

After a while Maggie cleared off the table and began setting up her coffee pot and a hose on the stove. She got out the stamp collection and surveyed how she might get one or two of them loose. Once the steam began coming out of her contraption, she brought one of the binders to the counter next to the stove.

"You don't have to do that," said Wyatt. It is probably a big waste of time."

"I don't mind. I feel like it."

After a moment the steam released a few of the stamps. Maggie laid them out on the counter and let them dry. Wyatt noticed her productivity. He went outside and was able to produce a longer piece of hose.

"Let's try this. It will reach further."

"Slick," said Maggie.

This allowed Maggie to leave the coffee pot on the stove while the hose reached the table, where she could sit and work more efficiently. After a while she had a couple dozen stamps loose and drying.

"I think I could do better if I had a bigger pot to make steam. I will work on it tomorrow," she said. She spent most of the evening pressing and flattening the loosened and curled stamps. She was pleased with how they came apart. Maggie found something soothing and satisfying in the task, like playing solitaire. Wyatt was impressed as well.

They sat next to each other at the table, working, with their arms touching and their voices flirting. The evening progressed, and they were very tired. They lay down in their bed. Maggie still had on her makeup, and Wyatt smelled like pomade. Wyatt touched Maggie's hand in sensual gesture. Maggie reciprocated turning to kiss him. They made love before going to sleep.

Wyatt awoke the next morning and got ready to go. He dressed and walked down the road a piece to where Mr. MacAnally's truck and trailer with the mower was parked. This would leave the pickup with Maggie, so she could go to town. Wyatt drove the rig to the location of the first yard to mow and completed the task. He reloaded the mower and headed up to the second one.

While driving to the second house he saw a billboard. "Restoration Dentistry. No Insurance? No Problem! Financing Available." Wyatt was interested. He moved his tongue in the empty space along his gum where the teeth were missing. He dreaded having to but wanted to talk to the dentist. He arrived at the second house and mowed the lawn as he did the first one.

Meanwhile, Maggie had gotten up and was preparing to go. She showered and spent much more time brushing and arranging her hair than she ever had before. She arranged it and curled the ends as best she could like the lady at the beauty shop had done. She opened the bag of make-up samples and applied the items. She left the house in Wyatt's pickup and first went to the Goodwill store.

She found a nice blouse and two summer dresses, each costing only a few dollars. She went over to the men's section and found two shirts for Wyatt. She walked by the pots and pans, thinking of her steam contraption. She found a small stovetop pressure cooker. It had a rattling weight on top that would allow pressure to build before being released. She examined it and saw that she could remove the weight and affix the hose she had used on the coffee pot. She paid for the selections and left. Maggie was good at stretching a dollar.

After that she decided to take the hair lady's advice, and she went to a small junk market where she had seen Mexican immigrants selling makeup. They were still there, and for only a few dollars, she found things similar to what the lady at the mall makeup counter had used. On her way home, she also stopped for a few food staples.

When Wyatt got home, Maggie had beaten him there. He walked in. She was wearing one of the dresses she bought and was connecting the hose to the new pot. She had made some biscuits. Wyatt took in this sight. The house smelled good. Maggie looked nice. Wyatt was pleased that she had taken to the stamp project. Wyatt walked up behind her to examine her improved contraption. She smelled nice. He reached down and tickled the small of her back flirtatiously. Maggie gave in to the affection. She turned around and hugged him. Their lips touched as he took her by the hand, and they walked into the bedroom.

A half hour later they returned, and Maggie resumed her steaming. She had everything connected, and a larger amount of steam was coming out. By the evening she had half of the first stamp binder done and had over a hundred stamps drying.

Wyatt sat quietly on the couch in postcoital contemplation. "I saw a sign for restoration dentistry today," he said. "I think I will go tomorrow."

"I'll go with you."

"You don't have to."

"I don't mind."

"I think it will be expensive, but I want to go see."

Not long after that, Wyatt retired for the night while Maggie steamed stamps awhile longer.

When Wyatt awoke the next morning, Maggie was already up and was pressing some dried stamps.

"I wonder if those things are worth anything?" asked Wyatt.

"I bet they'll be worth at least a little." Maggie had on her other new dress, and Wyatt put on one of the shirts she had gotten for him. Maggie fixed her hair and applied some of the flea market makeup. They got into the pickup and a short time later arrived at the building with the restoration dentistry sign. They walked into a waiting room full of posters of happy, white-toothed, smiling people. The secretary at the counter welcomed them.

"Are y'all here for a free consultation?" the secretary asked.

"Yes," said Maggie.

The secretary then gave them each a clipboard to fill out their medical information. Neither of them had anything to mention on the forms.

"Do y'all want to go separately or together for your initial consultation?" asked the secretary. They did not expect this option.

Maggie said, "Together."

"It will be just a moment." A few minutes later, they were ushered into a room with a few chairs. In walked a tall, middle-aged lady with a gleaming white smile. She sat down and tried to make the two customers more comfortable.

She started with Wyatt and asked him to smile.

"You have some yellowing. That is easy enough to fix, but the missing ones are due a partial denture. Implants are an option but can be expensive. The back ones look okay."

"Is that expensive?" asked Wyatt.

"Not too bad," said the lady. She then started on Maggie. "How are you Maggie?"

"Good. You?"

"I'm fine. Let's see what you've got."

Maggie opened her lips to reveal her off-color teeth.

"Your problem is mostly discoloration, which we can fix, but you have some decay in the back that must be addressed. That will require sedation and a small procedure."

"Is that expensive?" asked Maggie.

"Yes, it's a little more."

"What if we got a package deal?" Wyatt asked. The lady began adding numbers.

"Wyatt, yours would normally cost about two to three thousand." Wyatt was discouraged. "Maggie, yours would be more like three to four thousand." Maggie frowned. "But, if you do a couples' package, we could do it all for five thousand. We have financing, and you can make payments." Maggie assumed it was a no-go.

"When can we begin?" Wyatt asked.

"Next week," said the lady.

"Let's go for it," he said. Maggie looked at him, wide-eyed. She grabbed Wyatt's leg to pump the brakes on the expense. "We'll have to make payments."

"No problem. Lots of folks do."

A short time later, the lady produced a stack of papers for Wyatt to sign to guarantee payment. Wyatt and Maggie completed the forms and scheduled some appointment times, to begin on the following week's calendar.

"How are we going to pay for this?" Maggie asked as they walked outside.

"We will sell some stamps." Wyatt smiled.

"Yeah, right."

He did not know how they would pay for it yet. Maggie shook her head and got into the pickup. He usually only had a little cash, and she had not known him to be impulsive with what little money he had. He had a checking account, but it usually was empty. He also had a debit card, but it likewise usually sat idle in his wallet. Maggie realized he must have had this on his mind for a while. She felt strange accepting that he would pay for hers as well. She looked at him as he drove.

When they got home, the two of them set to liberating stamps and nearly finished the first binder. They had nearly two hundred stamps scattered and drying before they went to bed.

The next morning Wyatt went to mow some yards for Mr. MacAnally. Maggie took the pickup to the library to find some books on stamps to see if anything they had was valuable. She did find a book that was full of pictures of unique specimens. She recognized a couple, but the book gave no monetary numbers—only denoted that they were special.

When Wyatt returned home, Maggie had resumed her work on the stamps. Wyatt asked her what she had found out at the library. She told him. They spent the evening organizing and arranging the stamps from the first binder in an old catalog. The next morning Wyatt had no yards to mow. The two of them finished the second binder of stamps.

"We are going to have to find a place to sell these little bitches," said Wyatt.

"I wonder who would buy them?"

"I bet there is one of those dorky stamp shops in Nashville that might buy them."

"Let's try to find one."

The next day Wyatt had yards to mow. After he finished he stopped by a baseball card and comic book swap shop to inquire about any stamp buyers they knew of. He found out that there was a stamp shop south of the city. It was called Buy and Sell Stamps. When Wyatt got home, Maggie was almost done with the third binder. She had drying stamps everywhere. She had grown tired of stamps and was beginning to grumble.

"I found a place that might buy these," he told her.

She sighed. "Can we go tomorrow? I'm sick of them."

Wyatt agreed.

The next morning Maggie arranged the entire collection, now that it was free from its gluey prison. She had gathered every shoe box and empty container to put the stamps in to transport them. After a couple of hours' drive, they arrived to the stamp shop and went in with most of the boxes.

The owner was a short, balding man with a thin, nasally voice. He wore reading glasses on his nose and pronounced stamps as "staimps." He saw them come in and gestured for them to set the boxes on a table.

"Y'all got some staimps?" the man asked.

Wyatt and Maggie thought him humorous.

"Yes, sir. We have a few," said Wyatt.

"Yes, I see you have a 'few' there." They set the boxes down, and Wyatt went back to the pickup to get the rest of the boxes. Maggie opened the boxes for the "staimp" man to examine them. The odd man took his time and looked carefully at the collection. He mumbled in thin, squeaky tones as he did this. "You had to steam them apart, didn't you?"

"Yes," said Maggie.

"It happens often to these old collections. You did a good job." During the inspection the man sat three stamps to the side. Maggie did not know why they were significant.

"These three are special," he said. "These two are known for having uniquely small print. I'll give you one hundred dollars for them."

Maggie was surprised. "What about the others?" she asked.

The man continued to think and look at the specimens. "You've got some interesting pieces here," he said. "This collection is an old one. You could sell them individually and make more. Have you thought of that?"

"Not really," said Wyatt.

"I'll give you two thousand for the whole set," said the man.

Maggie was speechless.

"We'll take it," said Wyatt.

"You sound sure."

"We are," said Wyatt.

"Good. That's a good deal for both of us."

"Thank you," said Wyatt.

"How long have you been collecting staimps?"

"About two weeks," said Maggie.

"Ah, you inherited them?" the man asked.

"Yes."

The man gave Wyatt twenty one-hundred-dollar bills. They drove home in disbelief, laughing about their good luck and the odd man's funny way of talking.

A few days later, it was time to report back to the dentist's office. They both dreaded it. They arrived on time, and Wyatt was taken back first. Then a few minutes later, a person came and got Maggie from the lobby and took her back to a room.

A dentist came in to speak with Wyatt. "We are going to make a mold of your mouth in order to make the partial. After that, we will start on whitening."

Wyatt nodded.

"Do you have any questions?"

Wyatt said he did not.

"I'm going to be working on Maggie while you get this done," the dentist said. "She will take a little longer, and she may be drowsy when I'm done."

"Okay," said Wyatt, and the dentist left. A moment later a small-framed, smiling woman brought in a set of dental trays full of clay. She put the trays into Wyatt's mouth. They barely fit.

"Bite down," she said.

Wyatt did, and clay from the trays spilled into his mouth and down the back of his throat, gagging him.

"Just breathe through your nose," said the girl.

Wyatt's eyes were watering, and he was trying not to retch. A few minutes later, it was over, and the girl removed the trays and cleared the slobber from Wyatt's face. Next, she brought in another tray—this time a plastic one full of foam. The foam tasted funny, and he was told to hold still and not swallow. The girl then pointed a glowing blue light into his mouth that lit up the trays in ultraviolet blue. Wyatt sat still and followed directions. He could hear dental drilling coming from the room next door. He assumed it was Maggie.

Maggie had been given laughing gas as well as an injection in her lower gums to numb them. The dentist had to drill out some browning depressions close to the gum line, which had to be filled with polymer. Her procedure lasted about an hour and a half. When they brought her out to the lobby to join Wyatt, she was held up on either side by assistants. She was walking as if she were drunk. Her mouth was full of cotton, and her eyes were squinted in pain.

The girl behind the counter asked Wyatt if he would like to make a first payment before they left. He walked over and gave the girl $500 in cash from the stamps. She thanked him and told him just to be sure to make the minimum payment each month and that she would see them next week when they came back for round two. Wyatt nodded and held Maggie's hand and walked her to the pickup. She moaned as she got in.

On the way home, he stopped at a pharmacy drive-through and got Maggie's prescription filled. It came out in a small plastic bottle with pills inside. He opened it and gave her one. He brought her home and put her to bed. He sat on the couch, tired from the day. Maggie moaned and slept.

It was midafternoon. Wyatt thought about the events of the day. He pondered the fortuitous randomness of the stamp collection. He thought about his future. He thought about Maggie. He stared blankly into space. He sat quietly on the sofa with the old dusty clock sitting on the table next to him.

CHAPTER 7

A STICKY SITUATION

———◆———

THE NEXT MORNING MAGGIE FELT rough. She began sitting up and started more moaning. Wyatt brought her a drink of water and gave her another pain pill. She lay back down. He felt sorry for Maggie and would not leave today so he could be with her. About thirty minutes after giving her the pain pill, she got up out of bed and went hurriedly to the bathroom. It started out with her needing to pee but ended with her vomiting on the bathroom wall.

"I think those pills are making me sick," she said.

"You think so?"

"Yes. I'm not going to take any more." With that she went back to bed.

Wyatt went in to clean up the vomit. He finished the task hastily. He retched a couple of times doing it.

Maggie took no more pain pills and slept peacefully.

Trying not to make noise so that poor Maggie could sleep, Wyatt placed the boot box with the old journal inside on the table. He opened the box and removed a layer of decaying newspaper. Under the newspaper was a dry and brittle red-brown material that looked to be a cover of some sort. Wyatt tried to lift this, and a piece the size of a potato chip came off in his fingers. He set the piece aside and tried another. The next attempt resulted in the same, except that the piece was slightly larger. He did this four more times until he had what he thought was the cover removed.

Under the cover was a brittle and broken piece of what looked to him like ancient paper. Wyatt saw nothing that looked like writing. Wyatt tried to remove this, only to find it was more fragile than the cover. He also noticed when trying to lift it that it was indeed stuck to the pages behind it. He got the wise idea of trying to use a piece of monofilament fishing line to slide between the pages to separate them. This did have an effect. The top sheet was not as stuck as the other, and after wetting the monofilament line in his mouth, he was able to slowly and carefully separate some of the adhered areas. After moving the pieces away carefully and slowly, he did get the top wordless paper loose, only for it to break into three pieces immediately after he did so.

He sat the broken pieces aside with the broken cover and looked at the page underneath. He could not at first tell what was it said, but he knew there was writing on it. He began dusting it gently with his fingers. He could now make out words. The ink was faded. The words were large for hand-writing and had a line drawn through them. There were two sentences on the page, both drawn through. Wyatt looked at the letters and squinted. He went and got a pair of glasses out of a drawer, but they had some age and didn't help as much as they used to. He could make out the word *pension*.

Wyatt stood and fooled with a nearby lamp to throw more light on the mess. He also got a pad of paper and a pencil and sat back down at the journal. Wyatt squinted more and one time rubbed a bit of graphite on the marks, along with some spit. He began to scratch out words on the pad of paper. He looked at the puzzle and wrote down some words. He thought and looked and wrote more words. After about an hour he had written on his pad what he thought the two sentences said.

"I endeavor to complete this account of my response to the call for men to the First West Tennessee Regiment by Gov. Willie Blount on December, 1812, as pertains to eligibility for pension"

The other:

"I offer this account as fair and true. Please remit compensation upon receipt by editor."

What did this mean? Wyatt did not know. By the evening, Maggie got up again and this time was feeling better. She saw what Wyatt had been working on.

"Did you figure out what it said?" Maggie asked when she saw the exposed layer.

Wyatt showed her the writing on his pad.

"I wonder what that means," Maggie said.

"I don't know," Wyatt said. "The top sheet was not that hard to get off, but it broke. I don't know if I will be able to get any more apart."

Maggie sat down and took a look. She lifted slightly at the edge of the next page, but the corner crumbled as she did.

"Let me get the steamer," she said. Wyatt helped her assemble it on the stove, and soon a constant flow of steam was produced. Maggie began applying steam and touched the paper slightly with her fingernail. To her surprise the dampening effect of the steam rehydrated the page slightly and increased its turgor a bit. She took the monofilament line and began working it under the page. She added more steam. Going back to the fishing line, she moved it very slowly between the two pages. She moved more slowly than Wyatt had. Soon the page began to move freely. It did crumble in half at the final release from the page under it, but Maggie was pleased with her success.

She set the pieces aside and was taking stock of the new page it revealed. This one had more writing in the same large letters, but not just two sentences this time. They still could not make out what it said. Maggie began applying steam and a fishing line. This page was even more stuck and brittle than the previous ones. It took her longer to perform the extraction this time. When she had tired for the day, she had two pages separated. Although they had broken, the pieces were lying on the table ready to be deciphered, but they were just too faded. Maggie went back to bed. Her mouth still hurt.

Wyatt felt that Maggie would do a better job than he could do, and she would be more careful about separating the pages. She had already displayed aptness and

willingness. Besides, he did not find the tediousness interesting. He did not work on the journal while Maggie slept.
Wyatt sat down on the couch next to the old clock. Wyatt
took a midafternoon nap while Maggie slept and recovered.
An hour or two later, Wyatt awoke with a bit of energy. He
looked at the old clock next to him and decided it needed
some cleaning.

He got a small chair from the kitchen and set it next
to the small table by the sofa. He looked the clock over
and adjusted lights so he could see it well. The face was a
circular piece of wood with faded hours of the day printed
on it. It was not a fine piece, nor had it ever been. Its large
base provided most of the size and weight and was not
ornate.

Wyatt began rubbing the wooden top with a rag. The small pieces of wood that made up the top wiggled from being loose as he cleaned them. He decided he would take the top pieces apart and clean them, possibly oil them, and put them back together. The clock was of fairly simple design, and he figured it wouldn't hurt anything. So he did it. He carefully wiggled the pieces apart, gave them a rub and scrape, and set them aside. Soon he had all the top pieces removed, leaving only the large base.

The base was sturdy enough that he could pick it up. He picked it up and was going to shake some dust off it and also look at the bottom, when he turned it over that there was the slightest rattle. He shook the base and heard it again. Wyatt had assumed the base was solid due to its heaviness, but after shaking it again, he decided it definitely had something faintly rattling inside. He did not know how to get to the rattle. He examined the base more closely. He saw the base was larger at the bottom than the top and was formed from two pieces of wood. He estimated the rattle was coming from this joint. He had to separate the pieces.

He looked around and got a hammer and chisel from his toolbox. He placed the sharpened chisel at the faint seam between the two parts. He tapped it with the hammer. It did not budge. He applied the same technique to the other three corners. Finally he sensed a small amount of movement as the width of the line turned into the width of two hairs. He went around the corners again. This time there was more movement. After a few more times around, the two pieces were separating. When Wyatt got the top half loose, he sat it down on the floor next to the table.

Looking now at the bottom half of the base, he could see a depression had been carved into it, and it held a small, brown, folded piece of paper. Very gently, Wyatt lifted the brittle paper up and tried to unfold it. When he did it broke. He set the pieces on the larger table where the journal project was underway. On the paper he saw the same writing from the journal, except that it was smaller and not as faded. It read: "Deveraux's soap box is under the foundation stone of Chartres Mill. Take chain and mule."

Wyatt had no idea what it meant. He went to bed.

The next morning Maggie was up and feeling better. She saw the clock disassembled and was noticing the letter Wyatt had found as he walked in.

"What is this?" Maggie asked.

"I found it inside the base of the clock."

"Inside the base? How did you think to look there?"

"I took it apart to clean it." Wyatt was proud of himself.

"And it was just inside there?"

"Yep."

"What do you think it means?"

"I have no idea. Probably nothing."

"Who in the world would go to all that trouble of hiding a letter about a soap box in the base of an old clock if it didn't mean something?" Maggie asked.

"I don't know," said Wyatt.

Wyatt got ready to leave. He had a few yards to mow for Mr. MacAnally. While he was gone, Maggie was still quite intrigued by the letter. Maggie sat by the journal and stared at it. She looked at the two pages of the journal. She looked at the words written by a man two hundred years ago, but what did they say? The ink was too far gone and distorted by its gluey composition, having been stuck to the page in front of it.

The trailer in which she sat and thought was quiet, and the sun shone through the window. She closed her eyes. In her mind, she imagined holding the papers. She imagined she was holding them up to the window, and the sun shone through them. She opened her eyes as if lightning had struck. She walked outside and looked for an old screen door that was under the trailer. She found it. She dragged it out and cleaned it up. It contained two panes of Plexiglas that she wanted. Using some hand tools, she pried the old door apart and collected the two sheets of plastic window. She brought them inside and cleaned them. She took one of the panes and set it on the floor. She assembled the the unreadable pieces of parchment on the plastic. Once she had finished she carefully placed the other piece of plastic on top of it. She clamped them together using binder clips. When she lifted the two panes and placed them in front of the window, the sun shone through and lit it up like an amber lampshade. Just like in her daydream, the words on the page were slightly less faded, and the remains of the gluey ink were less hidden. Maggie could almost make out the letters. She could not wait for Wyatt to get home.

When he got home, she was wearing one of the new dresses and had on makeup. Walking in, he smelled the supper she had made. He walked over and kissed Maggie. She looked at him and smiled. The grass clipping stuck in Wyatt's pomaded hair made her laugh. She removed some of it. She thought he looked handsome.

"Go get cleaned up, and let's eat supper. I've got a surprise for you when we are finished." Maggie had never asked Wyatt to get cleaned up before. He liked that it mattered to her. He went and showered briefly and then sat down and ate the meal she had prepared. Maggie was smiling the whole time, and Wyatt knew it was about the surprise she had mentioned. He took his time to tease her.

When he had finished, he said, "That was great. Thank you. Now what is all this surprise stuff?" Maggie stood gleefully and moved Wyatt's plate to the counter. She then walked over and retrieved the two sheets of plastic from behind the couch. She brought it over to Wyatt. He looked at it and recognized the sheet from the journal but was confused as to why she had done this.

"What is this?"

"I'll show you." She walked toward the window and lifted the panes. "Damn it!"

"What?"

"There is no sun! You could see it! You could see it! I promise, Wyatt, you can see the words when the sun comes through! Damn it!"

"I've got you." Wyatt got up and took a lamp off the table. He turned it on. "Too dim," he said. He unscrewed the bulb and replaced it with a high wattage bulb from a work light. This time it was not too dim. The words Maggie saw now appeared.

"There they are," said Maggie.

"Maggie, you are a genius!" Wyatt kissed Maggie again. Wyatt propped up the contraption in front of the light and got his note pad. He began writing the words he saw and figured out the others assisted by their context:

"The likelihood had been confirmed by Mr. Grundy that the states and territories would soon return to the hand of the King. Redcoat victories in the north had emboldened their push southward. Eastern news prints told of crying mothers by the thousands whose sons were taken from the big boats and put into redcoat regiments."

They read the words on the page Wyatt had written.

"He is telling a story," said Maggie.

"Yep, sounds like it."

"Some of the words are scribbled and marked out."

"I guess he couldn't make up his mind how to say it."

"Let's do the other page." Maggie quickly removed the binder clips and carefully removed the fragments, replacing them with those of the next page. She reassembled the device and placed it in front of the bulb. Success again!

"Many had advocated for the militia and the state's men to move north and strengthen the failing effort. A call was sent to enlarge the state militia, and more regiments were to be formed. This was declined in the past as being too far to maintain a regiment."

They were out of sheets. Maggie fired up the steam contraption, and the two of them worked late into the night, freeing leaves of the journal. The work was long and tedious. It was frequently discouraging as some of the leaves crumbled when separated, making them a challenge to reassemble onto the plastic. It became obvious it was going to take some time to finish. After six more leaves were complete, they finished for the night.

Word went that Blount called for able men with experience to report to the militia. A large division was to be formed for northern excursions. Service would be exchanged for pension and land parcel compensation. In November 1812, a group of men gathered at Franklin County Courthouse and formed a regiment under Colonel Metcalf. The colonel was made aware of my service as aide to Colonel Huston in his Mounted Kentucky Regiment. Upon this I was appointed aide and captain.

I returned home and settled affairs and in December 1812, I left a wife and crying babe to accompany Metcalf to Nashville. We were distressed to learn the militia was not to head north but rather south to New Orleans. We were to join in branches with other units to go south into the lower territories to hold the Mississippi against Indians. All men who gathered were displeased with leading the unit south. Two captains requested dismissal to go north for units gathering there and were granted permission to go without issue by Metcalf himself, who wished likewise to be going.

Jackson communicated to the colonels that we were to travel west to Memphis, where flatboats were to be commissioned and moved south. I was to lead a detachment overland along the river and ahead of the flotilla and report any hostile persons or forces. In two weeks we reached Washington north of Natchez. Shortly, a lieutenant from the regulars brought word from Armstrong to disband.

Metcalf, distraught though he was, claimed Jackson to be livid with rage and waste. Furthermore, the encampment in Washington brought the cramping purges to whole companies. Jackson, in defiance, did not disband but marched back to Nashville. Much displeasure accompanied this trip. All manner of tarrings and featherings were plotted by the men upon those who would inflict this upon us.

After writing the visible words on his pad, Wyatt was getting bored with the process. He was not sure the letters would reveal anything interesting, and what they had was mundane. Looking at the remains of the journal, they realized they had a ways to go.

"Don't know if there is much reason to keep going," he said. "This stuff doesn't make much sense."

"I don't know. It's kind of fun, I thought." Maggie was disappointed Wyatt was not enjoying it. "Let's do a few more," she said.

Wyatt looked at the journal and saw the thickness of pages yet to separate. "What if we start on the back?"

He turned the journal over, and the red-brown cover was removed. They found the pages were hardly adhered, but they were blank. They removed a dozen or so blank pages. Wyatt was more encouraged as this part moved faster, and he realized the whole stack may not be stuck. They had just lifted one of the blank pages when they found a small letter-sized piece of thin, fragile paper that looked to have been put there later. It was written in a different hand in black ink and was not glued like the others. It read:

"This fall after harvest, I shall visit. We will travel to Chartres Mill and retrieve Deveraux's soap.

—Wm. Rolley."

"What does that mean?" asked Maggie.

"Hell if I know."

"Chartres Mill? Deveraux's soap? That's the same names from the letter in the clock, Wyatt."

Wyatt was silent, and he looked at the letter.

"Surely it means something, Wyatt."

"It could be anything."

"It would be weird if it were nothing."

"It is probably a couple of old men telling war stories."

"Why would the old man not be separated from the clock? You know it means something, Wyatt!"

"Let's do a few more pages."

Fifteen more blank pages were removed before the writing began. The pages in the back with writing were stuck like the others. Maggie fired up the steamer and resumed the arduous task as before. When they got six pages removed, they began assembling them. They noticed the letters were smaller, and there were fewer scribbles and lines marked out.

Our regiment was to continue our moonlight operations. We probed and dispatched their centuries nightly, while daytime was spent digging and fortifying. The night before Christmas saw an especially large and organized assault against the British. Many were killed and taken. This continued for a week.

The Tennesseans were moved to Chalmette under Carroll, and a great effort was made for ample trenches and breastworks. On the morning of January 8, the British attacked en masse. God's almighty hand was with us. The British had no fear of our rifles, and a cruel scene of death was revealed unlike any seen before. They made more attempts over the next days, but the lines held. All British commanders had been killed. We were soon exchanging prisoners as the British continued to retreat.

Many spoils and gold for bribes had been taken from the officers. This bounty was guarded near the McCarty house. At this time, an agent of the Baratarians who had accompanied Lafitte was discovered to have left in the night on horseback, loaded with all he could carry of the British gold. I was ordered to the McCarty house. When I arrived Jackson and Laffite were there. Jackson had informed me that a Mr. Deveraux had made haste with the spoils that belonged to Mr. Laffite. He then told Laffite that I was a trusted emissary and had served well for him. He asked that I pursue Deveraux and kill him on sight and return the property to Mr. Laffite. The gold was in Spanish coinage. I left without delay.

It was discovered that Deveraux was moving north. Two corporals and myself gave chase. Two days later we learned he had passed through a Dutch village and had left a few hours before. In the large prairie north of there, we saw him on horseback. We rode and dispatched him and brought his body and the two bags of Spanish gold he had taken. The man and the gold were returned to Laffite in New Orleans three days later.

Our regiment continued to monitor the English as they embarked. By March, the British had gone and the General released the city. I returned home the next week.

—Captain Barbee Collins
First Regiment, West Tennessee Volunteers, Metcalf Company

When he read the words, he couldn't breathe.

"Wyatt!" Maggie said. "The letter from the clock! The a box of soap! Do you think the journal and the letter from the clock fit together. Why would they hide soap?"

"I don't know," said Wyatt.

"It's not soap. They hid some loot. It has to be!"

"Maybe so."

"You think? Something they got from Deveraux?" asked Maggie.

"It kind of sounds like it."

"You think he meant to go back and get it?"

"Maybe."

"What if it's still there?" Maggie asked.

"Oh, it wouldn't be," said Wyatt.

"How do you know?"

"This was two hundred years ago."

"It might still be there."

"His buddies probably dug it up if it was still there."

"What if they didn't? Why wouldn't they have done it sooner? Maybe they never got the chance. That's why he held on to the clock like Uncle Luke said."

"Who knows?" Wyatt said.

"Someone should go look!" said Maggie.

"Meh."

"We should go look!"

"Look where?"

"Under the foundation stone of Chartres Mill is where!" Maggie exclaimed.

"And just where is Chartres Mill?"

"We could find out."

"The mill, if ever there was one, is probably rotten and gone," Wyatt pointed out.

"Well, whatever was put under it may not be," said Maggie.

"Soap? It probably sudsed up and washed away a century ago."

"It is not about soap! It can't be!"

"Well, maybe we will go look sometime," Wyatt said.

Maggie let it rest for the time being.

Over the next week, Maggie continued to think about the journal, the letter, and the soap. It couldn't be about soap, she repeated in her head, obsessing over it. When Wyatt worked mowing yards for Mr. MacAnally, Maggie stayed in the trailer, fixing meals and working on the journal. After a week she had finished it.

A couple of days later, a package was delivered for Wyatt. He was out mowing, and Maggie saw it was from the dentist's office and set it aside for him. When he arrived home, she gave it to him and was anxious for him to open it. When he opened it, he removed the partial set of teeth that had been made for him. He initially felt embarrassed for Maggie to see him put them in his mouth like an old man, so he went into the bathroom.

The device felt awkward in him mouth at first. However, when he smiled into the mirror, the new teeth filled the previous gap. He smiled bigger. He had not been able to smile without chronic fear of embarrassment or judgment that usually impeded his smiles since the accident in Havre. He opened the bathroom door. Maggie saw his red face hesitating to smile, so she smiled at him. He smiled back at her, revealing the full set of pearly whites.

"That looks nice," said Maggie.

Wyatt walked over to her to kiss her cheek. He felt his new teeth press his lips into her cheek and neck.

Maggie looked at him approvingly.

"I guess they will do," said Wyatt.

"How do they feel?"

"Fine."

"Well, you certainly have a much bigger smile when you let all of them show."

"Do you think I could grin down a bear like Davy Crockett?" asked Wyatt.

"I doubt a bear, but a possum for sure," quipped Maggie.

"Ha-ha, Davy Effing Crockett!" said Wyatt.

CHAPTER 8

THE SWAMP

———•———

IT WAS THE END OF September. Wyatt was mowing yards regularly, and Maggie stayed busy fixing and making things around the small house. Maggie had organized the sheets of paper onto which the Collins journal had been transcribed. She copied the letter in its entirety into a spiral notebook. She and Wyatt had both read it many times and were both unendingly intrigued about the journal and the odd letter about soap they had found inside of it.

One night after supper, Wyatt was feeling restless. He was looking at the letter in the green spiral notebook.

"Have you ever been down south Maggie?" Wyatt asked.

"Where do you mean by 'down south'?"

"Louisiana."

"Nope, I never have," Maggie said.

"I wonder what it's like."

"Hot and buggy, I hear," said Maggie.

Wyatt smiled. "We may need mosquito nets."

"Are we going there?"

"I don't know. I guess so. I kind of want to."

"Go in the pickup?"

"Yes."

"When would we leave?"

"Today is Wednesday," Wyatt said. "How about Saturday morning?"

Maggie gave no objections.

Wyatt mowed yards on Thursday and Friday while Maggie prepared for the trip. She planned a week's worth of quick meals in plastic bags. She filled jugs of water and packed blankets and towels. She improved their sleeping area in the back of the pickup and even made curtains for the camper shell. When Saturday came they got up early and hit the road with excitement.

They drove south through Huntsville. They then got onto the interstate and drove through Birmingham and Montgomery. They left the interstate south of Montgomery and took the road through the sandy cow country and peanut farms of North Florida. The sight of the sea and beach along the coast road from Panama City to Pensacola was their first view of the ocean.

"Look, Wyatt! It's the ocean," said Maggie.

"Yep, there it is," said Wyatt.

"It's not the color I expected, but it is still really pretty. I want to walk on the beach. But someplace that is not too crowded."

"That sounds good. Let's find a place," said Wyatt.

Wyatt drove the thin road along the peninsula that makes up Pensacola Beach. The water was a little bluer, and the sandy beaches were broader here than in other parts they saw. Dunes covered in sea oats swayed in the breeze from the waves. Farther down the road toward old Fort Pickens, Wyatt saw the familiar camping sign and pulled into an empty spot. The area was on the marsh side of the road, and there were a few palm trees to provide what little shade they could. Wyatt turned off the pickup, and the two of them got out.

They both inhaled deeply and tasted the briny flavor of sea air. They walked across the road to the beach, and they splashed around in the breaking waves.

"This sure is a pretty spot," said Maggie.

"Yep, it is," said Wyatt.

"I think I'm going to go back to the truck and get a towel and put on my bathing suit and sit on the beach."

They walked back to the pickup and got the beach supplies. Once they had what they wanted, they walked back to the sand. Maggie laid out two towels at the base of a dune that faced the cresting waves. Seagulls played overhead, and a long-beaked oyster catcher poked at the hidden critters in the sand. They watched the sun set before going back to the pickup for the night.

The next morning Maggie wanted to stay another day, so they did. Maggie brought an older one-piece swimming suit and put it on. Her pale, unsunned body shone while in the sun. Wyatt took the chance to walk up and down the waterline and through the paths in the marsh while Maggie lay on the towel, absorbing the sun. She moved only to roll over or to get a drink. She did not notice her skin turning lobster-red.

Wyatt had had his limit of sun exposure for the day, and the skin of his cheeks and ears was getting uncomfortable. He walked over to Maggie. When he approached she was facedown on the towel.

"Maggie, you had better wrap it up. You are going to burn. I think I have burned my face and ears already," said Wyatt. Maggie stretched her body as if to say she did not want leave this paradise.

"Whew, girl, your back is red! You are going to be hurting," said Wyatt.

She reluctantly stood up with her face up to the sun. "It feels good."

"You will see tomorrow," said Wyatt.

They went back to the pickup, and by evening Maggie was beginning to feel it. She slept with no covers that night, and by morning she was in pain and wanted nothing to touch her skin. She moved slowly out of the pickup, hissing and moaning.

"Man, you are red," said Wyatt.

"Oh, it hurts really badly."

"It looks like it." He walked over to feel her skin, but she pulled away from him.

"Oh, please don't touch me! It hurts too badly! I just want to sit in the truck." She moved slowly to the cab, all the while cringing anytime her skin moved or was touched.

Wyatt, somewhat amused, got into the cab and started the truck. The slight vibrations of the running motor shook Maggie's scorched hide, and she screamed.

"How in the heck are we going to move if you can't even stand for me to start the truck?" Wyatt asked.

"Just go slow, and don't hit any bumps!" said Maggie.

"This is going to be great!"

Maggie felt every bump in the road. Wyatt got onto I-10 that goes through Mobile, Biloxi, and past Gulfport. Before they got to New Orleans, Maggie could not stand much more.

"I think I need to walk around some. My burnt legs are killing me."

"Let's drive toward downtown New Orleans and walk around," said Wyatt.

Maggie agreed.

Wyatt followed the road signs to downtown New Orleans and the French Quarter. They parked in a large free lot and got out. Maggie felt better being on her feet but still could not bear to be touched. Darkness was approaching, and the lack of sun helped Maggie's skin to feel more tolerable.

"Let's walk around Bourbon Street," said Wyatt. Maggie followed him. The coming of night brought to life this city in which they were strangers. They walked down the streets of the French Quarter. Fun music filled the air. Revelers came in and out of the establishments. Lights from filament bulbs illuminated the vintage signs. The later the hour, the more active the streets became. At three thirty in the morning, they came to Waldenberg Park along the Mississippi River. Here they stopped to rest. When the light of dawn began to appear, they lay down in the soft grass on the bank and slept until morning came.

By noon the sun was warm enough that Maggie was ready to go back to the pickup. They walked back along the roads of New Orleans no longer darkened. They got some beignets before making it back to the pickup.

"Can we drive around and see more of the city?" asked Maggie.

"Sure," said Wyatt.

Wyatt drove through the grid of streets that make up downtown. When he got west of the city, the houses and live oaks grew larger and statelier. They soon came to the manicured grounds of Audubon Park and Tulane University. It was beautiful.

"Look at this, Wyatt. It looks like a giant flower garden. Let's get out and walk around," said Maggie.

Wyatt found a guest parking lot, and the two of them got out and began walking through the large, beautiful buildings of the Tulane University campus. They walked past the large School of Law building and past the School of Business. The library next to the history building was the most beautiful, with its shady paddocks around it.

"Let's go into this library," said Wyatt.

The library was cool and well lit when they walked inside. All types of people were moving in and around the books. They were looking diligently for hidden bits of knowledge in the pages. Wyatt wanted to look through the books. The vastness of the collection of books was intimidating. He had no idea where to even start or what to look for. Wyatt then noticed a tall student moving through the aisles of books, asking people if they needed any help. Wyatt observed him as he made his way closer to where Wyatt was standing. He could now see that something was wrong with this man. When he would speak, his body would jerk suddenly and his face would bunch up after every few words. The poor fellow had to fight to spit out every word, and with the words also came literal spit. Some of the students to which he was offering help declined out of obvious shock, but he persisted unaffected. He moved closer to Wyatt. The man now made eye contact with Wyatt and moved closer still.

"Heh...heh...heh...hello. Ca...ca...can I help you?" asked the man. The "ca...ca...caaa" sounded like a choking crow.

"Maybe," said Wyatt. "We are just looking, mostly."

"Har...har...are you students he...he...he...here?" He had no sooner said this than his chin and head jolted toward his chest three times.

"No, just passing through. Are you a student here?" Wyatt asked.

"Yep, I'm a his...his...his...toe...toe...history major. I just work here for financial aye...aye...aid."

Wyatt did not know how exactly to react to the poor man's squeaks and honks as he tried to speak. The man seemed to be ignoring the spells, so Wyatt supposed he should as well. Maggie also smiled politely.

"A history major? That sounds interesting. I wish I knew more about history," said Wyatt.

"Weh...weh...well, I do ta...ta...too. I hope to be a his... his...history professor."

"You know anything about the Battle of New Orleans?" Maggie asked.

"Shu…shu…shu…sure. Wha…wha…what do you want to know?

"Ah, nothing really. Except I was recently given an old journal of my great-great-great-great-grandfather's—or something like that. It apparently is his recollection of his participation in the battle. I wish I knew more about the places it mentioned."

"Tha…tha…that sounds interesting. I…I…I…could possibly hel…hel…help you with tha…tha…that. Do you have it with you?" the man asked.

"Well, not with me, but I have it in my truck."

"Bri…bri…bri…bring it tomorrow. I'll loo…loo…look at it with you."

"Where can I find you tomorrow?"

"Here. I…I…I…I get a lunch at noon. Meet me in the grove outside the library at noon, and I'll be…be…be… there."

"Thanks, man. I might just do that," Wyatt said.

"See…see…see you tom…tom…tomorrow."

"My name is Wyatt, and this is Maggie."

"Ni…ni…ni…nice to me…me…meet you. My name is Richard Pearle, but ev…ev…everyone calls me…me…me… Dicky."

"Well, I plan to see you tomorrow, Dicky," said Wyatt.

Maggie and Wyatt walked away toward the pickup.

"How about Dicky?" said Maggie.

"That was something. I don't know if I've ever seen a person stutter that badly before. I just tried to keep looking at him in the eyes while he choked out the words."

"What a poor fellow. I think you did okay," Maggie said. "Are you going to show him the journal tomorrow?"

"I guess we can. Do you mind staying in New Orleans another night?"

"No, I don't guess so. We can stop in a place and listen to some music for a while."

They made it back to the French Quarter and roamed the streets as they had done the night before. Maggie's sunburn had abated, and she no longer minded when Wyatt brushed his fingers on her back as they walked. She was wearing one of the light summer dresses she had brought. They walked leisurely through the streets. At about eleven at night, they walked to the end of Bourbon Street and heard horns and drums coming from an old bar named Fritzel's.

"That sounds good," said Wyatt.

"Let's go in there," said Maggie.

When they walked toward the door, a tall, thin, exotic woman with short, dark hair and a colorful dress like a girl on a cigar box greeted them. Speaking in French, she gestured for them to enter and follow her. She sat them down at a table in front of the band. The music was loud and lively.

"Do you want a drink?" the girl asked them. Wyatt was not twenty-one yet, but he guessed at midnight in New Orleans it did not matter. Wyatt also did not know what to ask for. He looked around and saw a man and woman sitting across from them, sipping a purple, fruity-looking drink.

"We will have two of those," said Wyatt pointing at the beet-red drinks.

"Two hurricanes?" she asked.

"Yes," said Wyatt.

A few moments later, she brought Wyatt and Maggie two hurricanes. They were thirsty and drank the Hawaiian punch and rum combination quickly. They both smiled as they experienced the light, floating sensation of their first alcohol buzz. A few minutes later, the tall lady returned.

"Two more?" she said.

"Yes," said Maggie.

The pair became tipsy and flirty as they swayed to the music and lights while their minds whirled. At three in the morning, they stumbled back to the pickup, climbed in, and slept in the back until morning.

Their heads ached when they awoke. Maggie felt the worst. Wyatt got out of the back first and went to get coffee. He brought it back to Maggie. Maggie was now stirring and was getting out of the back of the pickup when Wyatt returned.

"I see why folks don't do this every night. I think I am going to puke," said Maggie.

"I think some people do it every night," said Wyatt.

"Not me!"

"Let's head back to the library across town and see if Dicky shows."

"Poor Dicky," said Maggie.

They got into the pickup and drove back to the Tulane campus. They walked around more of the grounds until it got closer to noon. Maggie was carrying the green spiral notebook containing the Collins letter. When they made their way to the garden grove, they saw Dicky sitting at the table like he said he would be. He was eating a sandwich wrapped in a paper towel. They could see the hair on his head shake when his body jerked in spasms as he chewed. He was finishing the sandwich when Wyatt and Maggie came to his table and sat down.

"Hey, Dicky," said Wyatt.

"Hhrrnk...hhrnk...hey, Wyatt. You...you...you came back." Dicky's eyes clinched tightly together and released. His tongue leaped from his mouth, and he bit down on it. His stutter was worse today. "Di...di...did you bring the leh...leh...letter?"

"Sure did," said Wyatt. Wyatt sat it down in front of Dicky, and he opened the first page and began to read. His face stayed fixed as he turned the page.

"This is ki...ki...kin...kinda neat. A real fi...fi...find."

"Does it make any sense to you?" asked Wyatt.

"Shu...shu...sure." Dicky kept reading and turning pages. "This fella pro...probably wrote this a few years after the ba...ba...battle. These old off...off...officers could get money for sell...sell...selling their memoirs to pay...pay...papers. They also made accounts for pen...pen...pensions. I'd say that is what this is." He continued reading. Dicky reached into his back pocket and got out a pencil. "Woo...woo...would it be okay if fy...fy...fy...if I made you some notes?"

"Sure, please do," said Wyatt. Dicky began scribbling notes after the various names he read. He made notes about the names Grundy and Blount. He talked about the battles against the Red Sticks. It was the name Laffite that excited him.

"It looks li...li...li...like he met gshu...gshu...Jean Laffite. He is kind of a le...le...le...legend. He continued reading. "Prairieville," he said.

"What is Prairieville?" asked Wyatt.

"That's the name of the play...play...place now where he found Dev...Dev...Deveraux. The meadow. That would be Prairieville."

Wyatt and Maggie listened to and watched Dicky as he continued through the letter. "He was wi...wi...wi...with the Tennesseans at shall...shall...shall...Chalmette. Y'all could go...go...go see it."

After a while longer, Dicky had finished reading the letter and making notes. "You...you...you have something spe... spe...special. A rr...rr...real family air...air...heirloom," said Dicky as he handed the notebook back to Maggie.

"Thanks so much," said Wyatt.

"No...no...no problem," said Dicky.

Wyatt and Maggie walked back to the pickup in quiet contemplation, thinking about what all Dicky had said about the letter. They were especially intrigued about Prairieville or the meadow south of Baton Rouge.

"I wonder where this Prairieville is?" asked Maggie.

"I don't know. Let's look on a map."

"You think we can find Chartres Mill?"

"I don't know that, either," Wyatt said. "I hate to waste a bunch of time looking for something that likely isn't there."

"It won't hurt to just look," she said.

"I guess not. Let's see if we can find it."

"It might be fun," Maggie said. "Speaking of fun, what are we going to do tonight?"

"I guess we should drive around and find a place to stay," he said.

They did not head north toward Baton Rouge yet but instead headed west, away from the city and toward the swamps on the west side of the river. As afternoon approached, they saw signs for Lake Fausse Pointe State Park. Wyatt liked the sound of it and followed the signs to the entrance. He pulled the pickup next to the blue building on stilts where there sat a clerk for entrance into the park.

"How are y'all today?" asked a plump older woman.

"We are good," said Wyatt.

"Can I help you?"

"Yes, do you have any sites available?"

"Oh yes. It is not very crowded this time of year."

"Why is that?"

"It is a little buggy for city folks. We have to keep the screens closed because the mosquitoes get a bit violent at night. Y'all zip your tents tight when you go to bed."

"Hmm," he said. "I don't know about a skeeter attack. You think we ought to go someplace else?"

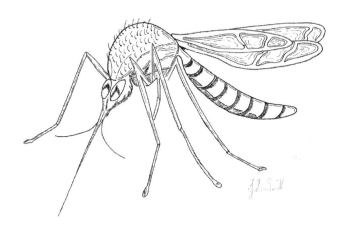

"Naw, hun. Just use repellant and keep moving when you go out of the tent."

Wyatt proceeded reluctantly as the lady gave him a slip of paper with his site number on it. He drove the truck down the narrow roads through the swamp park until he reached the site that was theirs. The whole place had once been a gator-laden lake that rose and sank over a few mounds of dry land. Additional piles of mulch had been added to the mounds to make them big enough for a tent. All manner of huge dragonflies and other smaller flying things bumped against the window and against their sweaty brows when they got out of the cab.

"Good gravy, Wyatt! We are going to be eaten alive by all these bugs!" said Maggie, waving the flying creatures away from her face as she coughed up the ones she had inhaled.

"Whew! They are thick! We are going to have to keep the camper closed," said Wyatt.

"What are we going to do until then?"

"The lady at the booth said to keep moving. Let's go for a walk."

Maggie gave no objections. They walked together at a swift pace, and they discovered that it did keep the bugs off their faces. As they walked down the camp roads, small furry creatures were abundant. Huge, squawking birds flew overhead, and butterflies the size of their hands landed on them.

"This is really something, huh, Maggie? How beautiful."

Maggie said nothing but swatted at the bugs and flicked the crawling ones off her clothes. "I don't know," she said, frowning.

They walked on farther. The road they were on began to fade into the edge of the woods. When they reached the end, they saw an entrance to a trail. There was a sign that read, "Scenic Swamp Trail."

"Look, Maggie. Here is a trail. It says two miles. Let's go on that."

"There is no trail there. It just goes into the water!" she said.

"There are reflectors on the trees. Look."

After a moment they heard a motor coming down the trail toward them. Shortly, a man on a four-wheeler came rolling out of the knee-deep water. He stopped when he saw the couple. The man ignored a huge swarm of mosquitos that were following the carbon dioxide of the four-wheeler's exhaust. When he came to a stop, the swarm gathered around his head, but it did not seem to bother him as he spit out the ones that went into his mouth.

"How are you two today?" asked the man.

"We are good," said Wyatt. "We were thinking about taking the swamp trail."

"You should. It's just busy as can be with critters, and it is quite a show," said the man.

"How deep is it?" asked Maggie.

"I think it is waist deep at the deepest part, but it is usually only ankle or knee deep in between the areas of dry."

"How do you know where to go?" asked Maggie.

"You just follow the reflectors. It is really easy at night when all of the reflectors light up from a flashlight."

Maggie cringed at the idea of going down the trail at night.

"Thank you very much. I think we might try it," said Wyatt.

"Good. Y'all have fun," said the man, and he drove away.

"I don't know about going at night, Wyatt."

"Oh, it will be fun. The man said it was easier at night. Let's go back to the pickup and think about it."

Darkness was approaching when they got back to the pickup, and the bugs were back at their faces. They trotted to the cab and got in to shelter themselves from the flying mass. Wyatt was already digging under the seat for two flashlights, excited for the nighttime swamp excursion. Maggie was not looking forward to it.

"Are you sure, Wyatt?"

"Yes, come on. We can't just sit here in the truck," he said.

Maggie whimpered.

"Ready?" he said.

Maggie figured it must be safe since the man suggested the trip. Wyatt would be with her and he had kept them safe so far. Giving her silent but reluctant approval, she grabbed the other flashlight and got out into the swarm. They moved briskly back to the trailhead. The reflectors were now very visible since the moon was out. Wyatt led the way into the knee-deep water and walked to the first reflector. He could hear Maggie sloshing and whimpering behind him.

"Wyatt, this is gross!" she shouted.

"It is fine. Just keep moving."

About three reflectors in, they saw a huge fat raccoon the size of a dog walk by, not seeming to care they were there. A large barred owl landed in a tree above them. Wyatt looked around in amazement. Maggie looked around in horror.

"Let's go back, Wyatt. This is too much," she pleaded.

"Oh, it will be okay. Let's keep going."

Wyatt was having a blast in the muddy water. He figured she would eventually get used to the critters and start to enjoy it as much as he was. He sloshed a half mile or so more with Maggie whimpering behind him when they came to a part of the trail that was on dry land.

"Look, Maggie. Dry dirt!"

"Thank God." Maggie's spirits lifted slightly when she walked along the dry path. This was only temporary, however. Suddenly the swamp was filled with Maggie's screams.

"Shit! Oh shit, Wyatt! Snake! Shit! Shit! Shit!"

Wyatt looked back in time to see a screaming Maggie in midair having just leaped over a copperhead that Wyatt had not noticed. Wyatt looked to see the small copperhead that had crept slowly onto the path. The copperhead barely noticed Maggie doing a quick over its tail to avoid stepping on it. Wyatt saw that the danger had passed and the snake seemed not to care. However, Maggie was terrified and was sprinting straight toward Wyatt. He braced himself, and she jumped onto his back. Maggie kept screaming and was crying. Wyatt was laughing. He hated to laugh but it was his turn, he thought the swamp was beautiful and magical. It was teeming with life and movement. However, Maggie was terrified. He placed Maggie's feet on the ground, trying to control his laughter.

"Why in the hell are you laughing? I just had to jump over a damn snake!"

"I'm sorry, I'm trying not to?" said Wyatt.

"I don't get it Wyatt, that snake was poisonous." she said.

"I know but he did not care to flips about you, but you sure shit your canoe over him," said Wyatt letting a few audible snickers escape.

"I don't think it is very funny, you said it would be okay, and I wouldn't call this okay."

"Let's keep moving," said Wyatt, smiling. He had stepped over a careless snake a few times playing around the creek as a kid and the episode had caused him only moderate alarm. Maggie did not share this perspective, and wished she had shown a few more objections when Wyatt talked her into the swamp hike. She could not now understand Wyatt's current calmness.

Maggie's whimpering was worse now. She screamed again when a lazy armadillo passed between her and Wyatt. Wyatt only laughed more. When the dry trail faded back into the swamp and the reflectors resumed, Wyatt pointed out three large water moccasins about twenty feet away to Maggie. Their heads were as big as Wyatt's fist.

"Maggie, look at those!"

"My God, Wyatt! More snakes?" She began sobbing. "I can't go any farther, Wyatt. This is crazy!"

Wyatt knew they were safe at their current distance from the huge snakes. He could not recall seeing water moccasins before as big as these were. He knew the sight of them would rile Maggie. "We have to keep going. We can't just stop," said Wyatt, still trying not to laugh.

Wyatt convinced her to keep going by not letting go of her hand as they walked the last mile of the swamp trail. Maggie had become numb to the occasional opossum or skunk strolling nonchalantly by. Wyatt made a point to be on the double lookout for snakes, at Maggie's request. It was the bugs, though, that tortured her the most. When the last stretch of trail came to an end onto dry land, her whimpers were suddenly replaced by muffled screeches and spits as a thumb-sized moth flew into her mouth. Wyatt held his lips closed with his teeth. When the trail finally ended, and the rough pavement of the park road began, Maggie moved into a run to get back to the pickup.

When she got there she grabbed a towel and a change of clothes and went straight to the bathhouse without speaking to Wyatt. Wyatt, chuckling and swatting bugs, trailed behind her after grabbing a towel for himself. Maggie was covered in mud up to the waist. Her hair was a giant fly collection. Her face was dotted with mosquito bites and striped with blood streaks from the ones she smacked. All of this was further smeared by tears.

They finished a quick shower, and Wyatt waited for her to come out of the ladies' shower. She did not speak but walked next to Wyatt as they fought their way to the pickup. They quickly got inside the back and closed the door tightly behind them. Maggie began to stuff socks and tissues into any crack or crevice a bug could possibly enter. Once that was completed, she commenced a slapping reign of terror against any and all crawling or flying things in the camper. She left no article unturned until she was certain there were no bugs inside. When she was satisfied, she lay down faceup on her sleeping bag. She was wearing a thin yellow dress that lay lightly on her skin. Her sunburn had also begun to crack and itch. This itching, mixed with paranoia, kept her on a hair trigger for a slapping spasm.

Wyatt, he lay low.

Soon they were asleep. A few hours of peace came, and all was going well. Maggie had done well at clearing the camper of bugs. However, on the outside of the camper crawled a fuzzy black caterpillar. It was crawling around the edge of the metal frame of the clear rear door. It came to a small cotton sock that had been stuffed into a corner. The caterpillar, being mostly fuzz, was slender in body and was able to squeeze through the folds of the sock and get into the camper with ease. It made its way down the inside of the tailgate, and because fate is cruel, it headed toward Maggie. For reasons only known to the caterpillar, it decided to crawl over the sleeping bag and onto Maggie's dress. It then came to the edge of the dress and began a journey up the inside of her dress, hanging upside down. This journey would end on the loose fabric betwixt her breasts, where it grew tired of hanging upside down. The fuzzy caterpillar decided to take its chances upright on the human skin beneath it.

Wyatt awoke to Maggie screaming like she was on fire.

"Snake!" screamed Maggie, followed by frothy panic.

"Where?" yelled Wyatt.

Maggie only screamed and tore for the camper door. After she got most of her body out of the camper, she began pulling the dress over her head. By the time her feet hit the ground, she had the dress off and thrown. Wyatt grabbed his flashlight to see Maggie slapping her naked body like a maniac in the moonlight.

Wyatt howled with laughter! "What are you doing, Maggie?"

"It was a snake. It was on me!" She pointed between her breasts.

"A snake?" Wyatt pointed his flashlight at the dress on the ground to see a three-inch fuzzy caterpillar crawling out of the pile of fabric. "There is your snake!" Wyatt laughed harder.

"This place is crazy, Wyatt! I'm not staying here. I'm leaving!"

"Okay. Okay. I'll get ready. But put some clothes on. Someone is going to see you out here slapping your tits like a crazy person in the dark." Wyatt could hardly hold it together.

Maggie, a shy and modest person, began whimpering again as she ran over to the dress and shook it out. She put the dress back over her head. She got into the cab and started the motor from the passenger side and waited for Wyatt. Wyatt did his best to breathe normally between chuckles and snickers. He remembered the ribbing he got from Maggie when he ate the pickled eggs and shit his pants, and he would also remember her running naked in the dark from a three-inch caterpillar. Wyatt got inside the cab and closed the door. Maggie began another violent bug-clearing assault on any poor thing that had flown into the cab. Wyatt cranked up the air conditioner and drove out of Lake Fausse Pointe State Park.

They drove north to Lafayette and then, getting back onto I-10, they drove toward Baton Rouge. They pulled off I-10 before getting to the city and napped in some shade. By midafternoon they were back on I-10. They passed Baton Rouge, and then the road took them south of the city and into the flat prairie. The town of Prairieville did take up this area, just as Dicky had said. They drove through Prairieville and saw nothing that caught their eye. Wyatt turned the pickup around and drove back through Prairieville. Going northwest again on the interstate, he saw a sign that said, "LSU Rural Life Museum." He took an exit and followed signs to the Rural Life Museum. It was a collection of old houses and structures that had been relocated to this spot.

Wyatt and Maggie got out to stretch their legs. They walked by the old post office and general store. He walked inside an old school. On its walls were plaques and photographs of the area and of various farming practices that took place there over the past two centuries. He walked over to a different wall. This wall had maps of various agricultural businesses from times past. One of these maps caught Wyatt's attention. "Agricultural Points of Sale, 1820–1830" was the title on the bottom left corner. This map showed the shaded area of farmland that made up the meadow south of Baton Rouge. It was marked with many types of businesses. There were red dots for livestock markets and sugar mills, smith shops, liveries, depots, loading docks, and feed mills.

Suddenly, he noticed a name on the map: "Chartres Mill." It was next to a red dot on the tip of a piece of land called Plaquemine Point that poked into the path of the Mississippi River. The fact that this Chartres Mill fit the time and location of the story in the Collins letter startled him. He went to get Maggie.

"Look at this, Maggie. Right on the tip of this point," said Wyatt pointing at the map.

"Chartres Mill. That is the name from the letter," she said.

"Yep, I think so," said Wyatt.

"Could it be?"

"I think it is possible."

"Can we go look for it?"

"I guess we can. I don't see why not," he said.

They got back into the pickup, and Maggie found the corresponding point on the Louisiana road map they had. Wyatt drove toward Plaquemine Pointe. As they drove along the river road, they passed a huge barge dock loaded with stacks of shipping containers. They continued farther and came to an area where the red dot and the name Chartres Mill had been on the old map in the museum. The area was a mass of trees and terraces that had obviously been flooded many times. Wyatt steered the pickup down a narrow dirt road toward the river. The road faded to nothing but a natural path west into the woods along the back of the Mississippi. Wyatt realized that much of the land on the map he saw in the museum had been washed away. There were U.S. Army Corps of Engineer signs. Wyatt and Maggie got out and walked down the path. The woods were mostly masses of driftwood gathered in huge clumps among large trees. They came to an area of several old stacked stones that were badly eroded and weathered from neglect. These stacks increased in frequency as they moved farther along the path. Eventually they came to where a gathering of old rock walls met the river. About two hundred feet from the river was a large square-hewn stone that obviously belonged to some old structure long worn away.

"What is that big rock?" asked Maggie.

"It looks like a big foundation stone. It must have been part of a loading dock for something."

The stone was about five feet wide and ten feet long. They did not know how tall it was as it had sunk into the ground. It also was partially covered by a huge mass of driftwood from a recent flood.

"This should be the spot on the map we saw in that old school," said Maggie.

"Yes, I think it should be," he said.

"You think it is still under there?"

"No telling. I doubt it, even. It is kind of crazy that we found an actual Chartres Mill that has a foundation stone, though, huh?"

"I guess there is no way to look under it?"

"No, we would need a backhoe," said Wyatt.

They looked around the area for a few more minutes and walked back to the pickup. Wyatt drove out of Plaquemine Pointe and then back onto the interstate. They drove until they reached Pensacola again, this time around midnight. They parked in the familiar spot and walked on the beach once more in the dark before sleeping. They drove back to the trailer house in Flintville the next day.

Once back home, Wyatt went back to mowing yards and Maggie to her domestic projects. She made Wyatt two shirts with contrasting buttons to go with his new pomaded hairstyle. Maggie had also been trying out some new hairstyles that she had seen people with in pictures in magazines. She was wearing light makeup regularly now, and was even talking differently. She had devoted herself completely to Wyatt and now thought of herself as half of a whole, though she did not articulate this to him. She usually had a meal ready for Wyatt when he got home from mowing. One evening a few days after they had returned from the New Orleans adventure, she had just finished cooking a small pork chop supper when Wyatt walked in. Wyatt was chipper, and Maggie was flirty. Maggie had also been thinking about the large square rock at Plaquemine Pointe.

"How is supper?" she asked.

"It is great. Thanks for making it," he said.

"No problem. Any trouble today?"

"No, no trouble."

"You know that mess of sticks and junk blocking the way to that big rock we looked at?"

"Are you still thinking about that rock?" asked Wyatt.

"Maybe. You know the junk I'm talking about?"

"Maggie, there can't be anything under there. It is going to be a huge waste of time and a big pain in the ass to even try to look under that rock."

"You don't know that it would be. I don't think we would need a backhoe. I think we could move it with axes and shovels."

"Plus, it is probably trespassing!" said Wyatt.

"No, you saw those Corps of Engineers signs, its puplic.

"Maggie, that is crazy!"

"Why do you say that?

"That is hours of work you are talking about!"

"Yes, I know. That's why we need to have all the tools with us. We will need a pickaxe as well."

"Maggie! You are planning on going back there, I take it?"

"Why not?"

"It's a huge undertaking!" Wyatt said.

"Nah, it will take all night," said Maggie.

"All night?"

"Yes, we can do it in a night. We will need some good flashlights."

Wyatt sat silently and absorbed what Maggie was suggesting. He supposed it was possible, but he was certain it would be a waste of time. But the remote possibility of something being there maintained the fire of curiosity in both of them.

"In a night?" said Wyatt.

"Yep, I bet we can," said Maggie.

Wyatt huffed, and Maggie smiled.

Four days later they were back on the road in the pickup headed to Plaquemine Pointe. Wyatt was still frustrated that the task ahead of them would likely be all for naught. He felt foolish. In the back of the pickup, along with the sleeping bags, were two axes, two shovels, a pickaxe, two lanterns, a length of chain, and a cable winch. They left Flintville early in the morning and reached Baton Rouge by night. They stayed in a Motel 6 on the edge of the city and resumed the trip to the point the next morning. By noon they were back at the remains of Chartres Mill. There was not a soul to be seen, and the busy barge port was a ways away. They began clearing brush and debris from the stone. Wyatt got an axe and he and Maggie began loosening the large branches in order to clear them away from the stone so the digging could commence.

It took a couple of hours before they had cleared away enough mess to get access to the soil in which the foundation stone had sunk. Maggie already had a blister on her right thumb that was stinging. The task now was an immense one: to dig. Wyatt started with the shovel, moving away the dirt and roots to find the bottom of the stone. Another two hours later, he discovered the stone was about two feet thick. He dug a huge gravelike pit in front of the stone in order to begin tunneling under it. He was already tired and getting blisters. Maggie took a few turns with the shovel and pickaxe, but tired quickly and became discouraged from the pain of her blister after only a few swings.

After three more hours, they had made a dent in the earth under the edge of the stone. Wyatt figured that in a couple more hours, they could dig to where someone could have buried something under it if they had wanted to. The problem was that he was exhausted. The sun was faded, and Maggie would have to hold the flashlight while Wyatt pushed on. Maggie wished there was more she could do to help.

"I could take another turn," said Maggie hoping to help.

Wyatt remembered the quick handle burn she got after only a minute of digging. "There is no reason for you to tear up your hands, you holding the light is helping," he said.

When the hours passed, and he felt he could go no further, Wyatt had cleared enough dirt from under the rock that if anything were there, he would have found it. Discouragement was mixing with exhaustion, resulting in growing frustration when he swung the pickaxe again. This time, however, the pickaxe did not rebound against the hard, rocky dirt as it had before. Instead, the dirt gave way a little. Wyatt picked up the pickaxe and swung again, and the dirt gave way more. Wyatt got down on his knees in the light to see what was there.

"What do you see?" asked Maggie.

"It is soft here." Wyatt's voice was feeble with exhaustion. He was struggling to dig in the soft dirt because his arms were spent.

"Let me down there. Hold this light," said Maggie. Wyatt leaned back against the wall of dirt and made room for Maggie to squeeze in to probe the soft cavity of dirt Wyatt had just found. Maggie scraped away at the soft dirt with her hands. There was something there. She pulled out a handful of soft mush that looked to be rotten wood. The next few handfuls revealed the same. Another handful pulled out what looked like a piece of decayed canvas, followed by more handfuls of dirt. After a minute or so, she had removed most of the layers of dirt from the cavity, and she was feeling around in the loose dirt at the bottom. In the dirt, she felt a small, heavy, disk-shaped object. She picked it up and turned around to shine it under the flashlight Wyatt was holding.

"What is this?" she asked while rubbing the dirt off it. "It's yellow. It's gold-colored! It's gold, Wyatt!" She held it out to Wyatt.

"Well, I'll be damned! It sure is! Hellfire! Are there any more in there?"

Maggie began feeling around the cavity and produced two more. She felt around for quite a while longer until she was certain there was nothing else there.

"It's just those there," she said.

"Well, hell! Three gold coins aren't bad!"

"Wipe them off. What do they look like?"

They were large, silver-dollar-sized coins with numbers and letters around the edge. There was a shield and crown on one side and a cross with a banner around it on the other. They climbed out of the hole and looked at the coins more closely while standing. They gathered the tools and lights and put them in the back of the pickup and drove off. They drove to the same Motel 6 where they had stayed the night before. Once they got inside the room, they cleaned the coins and tossed them around to each other like school kids.

Once they arrived back in Flintville, their lives returned to how they were before they left, except that the gold coins sat on the table like prized ornaments.

"How much do you suppose these are worth?" asked Maggie.

"I'd say their weight in gold would put them at two to three hundred dollars each," he said.

"Surely they are worth more than that. They are old. They say '1715' on them."

"Yeah, that is what I was thinking. A collector would probably give us more for them," he said.

"Where would we find a collector?"

"That I don't know. We will have to find one," said Wyatt.

The next day, while asking around, they learned of a coin shop in Chattanooga. On a Tuesday morning, they drove to Chattanooga. The shop was named Choo-Choo Coins after the town's iconic trains. When they walked into the shop, they saw a few hundred gold coins in glass cases. A short, middle-aged man greeted them.

"How can I help you?" he said.

"We need some advice," said Wyatt.

"Sure, I'll try," said the man.

"We found these coins and want to know what to do with them." He set the three coins on the counter in front of the man.

"Oh, wow!" the man said. "These are fine old Spanish coins. These are spectacular because they are poured instead of stamped, like most you see. These are quite valuable. Where did you find them?"

"We dug them up," Wyatt said as he smiled.

"Well, that is a heck of a find. You are going to want to sell these to an antiquities dealer."

"Antiquities dealer? Where is one of those?" asked Wyatt.

"I think Atlanta is the closest one."

"What is the name of it?"

"Let me see if I can find the name of it." The man returned a few moments later with a name and address for European Antiquities and Imports Inc. Wyatt thanked the man, and they drove back to Flintville.

"Wyatt, these things may really be worth something," said Maggie.

"I know. That's what the fellow seemed to be saying," said Wyatt.

"Are we going to Atlanta?"

"I guess we'll have to."

On Friday they left for Atlanta. Maggie entered the address given to them by the man at Choo-Choo Coins into the GPS on Wyatt's phone. They hit some traffic, but six hours later they were close. When they got close, Wyatt parked the pickup in a nearby pay lot. They walked into the downtown building. The antiquities dealer was on the second floor. When they got off the elevator, they walked into a lobby filled with old statues and paintings. They walked to a counter where a young woman asked to help them.

"Yes. We were advised to come to talk to y'all about some Spanish coins," said Wyatt.

"Oh sure. You want to speak with Marcel. I'll be right back," said the girl as she stepped from behind the counter.

A few moments later, she returned. A tall, dark-haired man with a French accent and a pinstriped suit came out and walked toward them.

"Hello, I'm Marcel Dupree. How may I help you?"

"We have some coins we would like you to look at," said Wyatt.

"My pleasure. Do you have them with you?"

"Yes." Wyatt reached into his pocket and pulled them out, displaying them in his hand to Marcel.

"Hmm, I see. Let's go into my office."

He walked them back behind a wooden door into his large office filled with rare trinkets, statues, swords, and paintings. "May I hold them?" Marcel asked.

Wyatt handed the coins to him. He sat at his desk holding the coins and looked at Wyatt and Maggie.

"What do you think of them?" asked Wyatt.

"Very impressive," said Marcel. "Do you have any idea of what you have here?"

"No, not really," said Wyatt.

"These are a treasure hunter's dream. Congratulations. You could be famous."

"So they are valuable?"

"Oh yes. Extremely. How did you get them, may I ask?"

"We dug them up," replied Wyatt, not giving more details.

"The coins are called Tricentennial Royals. They were minted for the king of Spain in 1714. He probably once held these. They would sell at auction for several hundred thousand each."

Wyatt was pale and couldn't swallow. He was sure he had misheard.

"Did you say a hundred thousand each?" asked Maggie.

"Yes, the total would be well over a million," said Marcel.

Wyatt and Maggie began sweating.

"The problem is that their sale would attract lots of attention," Marcel said. "This would be necessary to get a good price at auction. How they were obtained will have to be published. You see, these would be very easy to steal. Will you be able to tell me how you got them?"

"I guess so," said Wyatt.

"Please." Marcel sat back in his chair and waited for Wyatt to speak.

"Well, a couple of months ago, I was given a journal of a distant relative. It included a tale of one of my patriarchs being ordered by Andrew Jackson to retrieve some Spanish coins a man named Deveraux had stolen. He said he recovered them and returned them to Jackson. Then we found a letter saying something was left behind at a place called Chartres Mill. When we went to Baton Rouge, we found a map with the location of Chartres Mill on it. We went and looked under the foundation stone that was mentioned in the letter, and there they were."

"Where is the location of this Chartres Mill?" asked Marcel.

"It is mostly washed away and all that is left is a big rock on some Corps of Engineers Land. The place is called Plaquemine Pointe, I think." said Wyatt.

Maggie, who had been standing next to Wyatt, walked over to a vintage map of the U.S. in a glass frame hanging on the wall. "Here," she said meekly pointing her finger at the bend of the river along the river she recognized.

Marcel now looked at Wyatt and Maggie with disbelief. "If what you say is true, more congratulations are warranted. You are just a typical treasure hunter with incredibly good luck," said Marcel.

"Will we have to prove it?" asked Wyatt.

"Yes," said Marcel. "Do you have the journal and letter?"

"Yes, we have them at home."

"Good. Will you be willing to sign an affidavit about how and where you found them?"

"Yes, sure."

"Your relative who retrieved these coins most likely saw these in a group of lesser coins, and because there were three of them, he figured no one would miss them. Also, they wouldn't have been as valuable then, when they would have been worth only their weight in gold, as they are now. Now, however, they are valuable because there were only a handful of them made for the king of Spain himself. What an incredible story they could tell if they could speak."

"That is incredible," said Wyatt.

Maggie said nothing, but her face was red and sweating with excitement.

"Yes," said Marcel in his French accent.

"When do you think we would be able to sell them?" asked Wyatt.

"Are you in a hurry?" asked Marcel.

"Not a big one, but they are for sale."

"Do you want to sell them to me?"

"Is that an option?"

"Perhaps. If you can provide the documentation, I could buy them. I would in turn sell them at auction for a profit, but the sale would need to be promoted and hyped to elevate the price."

"How much would you buy them for?"

"Hmm. If you are able to provide the journal and swear an affidavit that what you say is true, I would give you a million for them."

"One million?"

"Yes."

"What is the next step?"

"Are you going home today?" asked Marcel.

"Yes," said Wyatt.

"Take them home, and don't let them out of your sight or tell anyone you have them. In two days another gentleman and I will come to you with the necessary paperwork and a check, as long as what you say holds true."

"Two days?" asked Wyatt.

"Yes," said Marcel.

"And you will come to us?"

"Yes."

"Well, okay," said Wyatt.

"Good. And congratulations again," said Marcel.

"Thank you." Wyatt and Maggie stood, and Wyatt put the coins back in his pocket. They shook hands with Marcel, and Wyatt gave him the address. He confirmed again that they would speak again in person in two days. Wyatt felt sick to his stomach.

"Thank you, Marcel. See you in two days," said Wyatt.

"You are welcome. Remember, Wyatt, don't tell anyone you have them. Many treasure hunters like you are not as honest as you are."

On the drive back home, Wyatt and Maggie were in disbelief. Their minds were on fire.

"A million dollars, Wyatt!" said Maggie.

"Yep, that is what he said."

"In two days."

"You think he will show?" asked Wyatt.

"Sure. You think he won't?"

"I don't know. It sure seemed kind of fast and weird," he said.

"You think he was a flake and was lying to us?"

"I guess we will see in two days."

They couldn't sleep for the two days. Could Marcel have been a crook, or was he telling the truth? Wyatt had decided he must be a crook. They weren't sure either way until two days later, when a gray Cadillac pulled up next to the trailer house. Marcel and another gentleman got out of the car and came to the door. Marcel knocked, and Wyatt opened the door. Wyatt knew Marcel was going to kill them and run off with the coins.

"Hello, Wyatt," said Marcel.

"Hello, Marcel. It is good to see you," said Wyatt.

"Wyatt, this is Fred Lutz. He is an attorney. He will file the paperwork."

"Hello, Wyatt," said Fred.

Wyatt ushered them inside. Marcel saw the coins on the table and walked over to them and stood quietly staring at them.

"Wyatt, may I see the journal you mentioned?" asked Fred.

Wyatt showed him the remains of the old journal. He got out the chips of the old parchments that contained the original journal puzzle. He showed them the old clock and the hollowed-out space in it where the letter about Deveraux's soap had been placed. Wyatt also showed them on the Louisiana map where they had dug up the Tricentennials. Fred listened intently and wrote down what Wyatt was saying on the blank affidavit. After a series of questions, Fred seemed satisfied.

"We were very lucky," said Marcel. "Sometimes these finds have to go back to whomever owns the dirt from which they were taken. Fred did some checking, and that site is apparently now public and apparently metal detectors are allowed. So, even though you did not use a metal detector, I think you are good."

"So that settles it?" asked Maggie.

"I think this will pass as a valid find. They appear to have been obtained legally. Congratulations," said Fred.

Wyatt signed the affidavit, still staring back and forth between Fred and Marcel and wondering who would pull a gun first. Marcel got a checkbook from his pocket and began writing on it. A few seconds later, he tore off the check and handed it to Wyatt. Fred also had a bill of sale, and he took photographs of the coins.

Wyatt held the check in his hands. It was for one million dollars. He handed the check to Maggie. Her hands shook as she looked at it. Marcel picked up the coins from the table. Now they were his. He smiled with great accomplishment. Fred and Marcel exchanged pleasantries with the dumbfounded Wyatt and Maggie for a few more minutes, but they were in a hurry and soon left with the coins in the Cadillac.

Wyatt and Maggie stood on the porch holding the check.

"This is a damn check for a million dollars!" said Wyatt.

Maggie was crying.

"Let's go to the bank," Wyatt said. "I don't trust them. I think we have just been robbed."

"I know, it is too unbelievable to be true."

They got into the pickup and headed toward the branch of Bank of America that held their current checking holdings of about four hundred dollars. Maggie and Wyatt walked in the door. Maggie was holding Wyatt's arm.

The teller saw that Maggie had been crying and was very anxious about something. The teller thought the situation odd.

"Can I help you?" she asked.

"Yes, I would like to deposit a check," said Wyatt. He handed the teller the check. She held it and looked at Wyatt for a moment. She got up and took the check to the branch manager, who sat at his desk. The manager looked at the check and at Wyatt and Maggie, and then he picked up the phone and dialed a number. He was soon speaking to some-one on the other end. After a few minutes, he hung up and nodded his head to the teller. He looked again at Wyatt and Maggie.

The teller then walked back to her window where Wyatt and Maggie were standing. "Into your regular checking?" the teller asked.

"Yes, please," said Wyatt.

"Would you like a receipt with your balance?"

"Yes, please," he repeated.

She processed the check and gave a slip of paper to Wyatt that said at the end, "checking balance $1,000,427.30."

"Thank you," said Wyatt. He and Maggie walked out of the bank and got back into the green pickup to head home.

At the window, the teller and the bank manager watched them drive off.

CHAPTER 9

THE JOURNAL OF BARBEE COLLINS

———◆———

THE FOLLOWING ARE THE CONTENTS of the journal of Barbee Collins, with footnotes added by Dicky:

The likelihood had been confirmed by Mr. Grundy[1] that the states and territories would soon return to the hand of the king.[2] Redcoat victories in the north had emboldened their push southward. Eastern news prints told of crying mothers by the thousands whose sons were taken from the big boats and put into red-coat regiments.[3] Many had advocated for the militia and the states men to move north and strengthen the failing effort. A call was sent to enlarge the state

---

1 Felix Gundy was a US representative and a state representative for Tennessee from 1811 to 1829. He became a US senator from Tennessee in 1829. He was appointed US attorney general in 1838.
2 By 1813 successful British military campaigns on the Canadian border had nearly guaranteed colonial return to England.
3 British conscription of American sailors into the British Royal Navy was a frequent nidus for the conflict.

militia, and more regiments were to be formed. This was declined in the past as being too far to maintain a regiment.

Word went that Blount[4] called for able men with experience to report to the militia. A large division was to be formed for northern excursions. Service would be exchanged for pension and land parcel compensation. In November 1812, a group of men gathered at Franklin County Courthouse and formed a regiment under Colonel Metcalf. The colonel was made aware of my service as aide to Captain Huston in his Mounted Kentucky Regiment.[5] Upon this I was appointed aide and captain.

I returned home and settled affairs, and in December 1812, I left a wife and crying babe to accompany Metcalf to Nashville. We were distressed to learn the militia was not to move north but rather south to New Orleans. We were to join in branches with other units to go south into the lower territories to hold the Mississippi against Indians. All men who gathered were displeased with leading the unit south. Two captains requested dismissal to go north for units gathering there and were granted permission

---

4 Willie (pronounced "Wiley") Blount served as governor of Tennessee from 1809 to 1815.

5 Mostly involved in Indian conflict, Captain Huston (different from Colonel Sam Houston) led a mounted cavalry unit from Kentucky consisting of volunteers.

to go without issue by Metcalf himself, who wished likewise to be going.

Jackson[6] communicated to the colonels that we were to travel west to Memphis, where flatboats were to be commissioned and moved south. I was to lead a detachment overland along the river and ahead of the flotilla and report any hostile persons or forces. In two weeks we reached Washington north of Natchez. Shortly, a lieutenant from the regulars brought word from Armstrong[7] to disband.

Metcalf, distraught though he was, indicated Jackson to be livid with rage and waste. Furthermore, the encampment in Washington brought the cramping purges to whole companies.[8] Jackson, in defiance, did not disband but marched back to Nashville. Much displeasure accompanied this trip. All manner of tarrings and featherings were plotted by the men upon those who would inflict this upon us.

After returning to Nashville, we were given new orders to engage the Creeks, as they had reignited their attacks and were plaguing the entire populace. We reorganized and headed south. Following their bloody path, we engaged and dispatched small bands

---

6 Andrew Jackson was then the general of the Tennessee Militia.

7 John Armstrong Jr. was secretary of war, newly appointed by Madison in January 1813.

8 Dysentery was a constant plague of the army for the entire duration of the war.

of Creeks. Tecumseh[9] from the north had anointed the creeks as Red Sticks and under Weatherford[10] slaughtered men, women, and children. All persons were to move into fortifications. Engagements against the Red Sticks continued with regularity through the summer. Jackson was summoned to Nashville as the engagements continued.

September brought news. Jackson had been shot by Jesse Benton[11] and nearly lost an arm, and the Red Sticks had killed scores of women and children at Fort Mims.[12] Men wept when they thought of Fort Mims, and a burning hatred raged inside them. General Coffee[13] sent orders to move south. We had many engagements with the Red Sticks and dispatched them with regularity.

We were ordered back to Nashville in October and were reorganized. The main group was to move

---

9 Tecumseh, the great Shawnee chief, rallied natives of all tribes to unite against the Americans.

10 William Weatherford, also known as Red Eagle, was a Scots-Creek leader of the Creeks during their uprising.

11 Jesse Benton was the brother and second to Thomas Hart Benton (later a US senator), with whom Jackson had an ongoing feud.

12 On August 30, 1813, a force of Creek Indians belonging to the "Red Stick" band led by William Weatherford attacked Fort Mims in Alabama. Nearly five hundred militia men and settler families were killed or captured.

13 John Coffee, then general of the Tennessee Militia, was a lifelong associate of Andrew Jackson.

south with General Carroll[14] during the day, but our regiment moved at night and reported engagements to Carroll the next morning. Jackson told us he had an affinity and trust for our boys and would prescribe most perilous reconnaissance soirées.

Red Sticks were not given to organize and form ranks and were easily dispatched by rifle at a distance. In November at Tallushatchee, I led the company to count Creeks killed by Coffee's Cavalry.[15] Among them were women in warrior's paint. At this time a corporal brought to me a young Creek boy spitting milk. Christian sympathies were aroused at this sight, and men took shifts soothing the thing, including Metcalf's aides. Word got to Jackson of the Creek boy, and orders were given to deliver the babe to Jackson for inspection. I did take the boy to Jackson. This was my first audience with the general. I recall Jackson unswaddling the boy and inquiring as to the circumstances of his abandonment. He also then inquired of my previous history with Huston in Kentucky. I recalled to him my service as aide. He sent me to bring a woman he had seen cooking in the Negro regiment. I knew the one, and she came to the general's tent with no pro-

---

14 William Carroll was also a general in the Tennessee Militia and would later become governor.

15 The Battle of Tallushatchee was fought on November 3, 1813, in Alabama, between "Red Stick" Creek Native Americans and US Cavalry Force Brigadier General John Coffee.

test and took the babe in disbelief. I was dismissed after a time but did see the infant alive and being paraded about by Jackson and the regular officers.

After two weeks, I was given orders by Metcalf to return to Jackson's camp, to which I answered with trepidation. The general told me over table and bourbon that he had discussed my service with Metcalf and the circumstances of the Creek boy. To my unbelief he ordered me to accompany the Negress and the infant, along with a letter, to his home east of the capital and to deliver the Negress and infant to Mrs. Jackson. An opportunity for my rebuttal was not made.

The next morn, with little issue, the Negress and I rode north toward the capital. The Negress gave no trouble and complained little, despite her poor charge's unending screams, spits, and scours. After a ride of two weeks, the party made the gates of the general's planting outfit. My militia insignia allowed free pass by the foremen to the house. The fatigued Negress and foul smell of the boy were nearly turned away were it not for a head man at the house who recognized the letters I bore. He stated that it was more the familiar misspellings that proved authentic, rather than the signature, which could be made by any man.

After a time, I did observe Mrs. Jackson view the letters and, with paleness of face, she ordered the babe to be cleaned and taken in.[16] The head man informed me that the month prior a Creek boy had been received but did not survive.[17] I was offered hot water and overnight quarter. I recall the fine house. It was decorated for the New Year. Upon saddling the next morning, I did see a housemaid singing to the infant, now in clean, white swaddling. I left to return south to the regiment without delay.

I made report for Jackson, who heaped words of praise and indicated I would be recalled to front special needs as they arrived if I were agreeable. I affirmed. I rejoined Col. Metcalf and the lieutenants of the company. By March small engagements had congregated the Red Sticks along the Tallapoosa River. Metcalf gave instruction that our regiment was to engage and flee from the Red Sticks at intervals to consolidate them in a marked bend in the river found by Coffee's mounted scouts, where they could be dispatched in numbers.[18] Metcalf asked our com-

---

16 Lyncoya Jackson was born to Creek (Muscogee/Red Stick) parents and was orphaned during the Creek War following the Battle of Tallushatchee. He was brought to Jackson's home, The Hermitage, in 1813. He was to attend West Point Military Academy but died at age seventeen due to tuberculosis.

17 Records indicate Jackson attempted to adopt a previous Creek boy, but it did not survive. This was not an uncommon practice for ranking officers.

18 This likely refers to the Battle of Horseshoe Bend, when Creek Indians retreated into a bend of the Tallapoosa River and were annihilated on March 27, 1814.

pany to repose during the day in order to engage the Red Sticks at night while our mates engaged at day. This would add to fatigue and encourage chaos among the Red Sticks. The effort was effective.

Despite their assembling a breastwork, the bend of the river left them open to rifle and cannon. They were no longer a source of issue after Coffee's riders advanced. Houston,[19] then still a lieutenant, led the charge and was a casualty, but he did survive and receive much praise from Jackson and the colonels. This was also the time the Red Sticks' white chief, Weatherford, marched into camp and held formal parlay with Jackson.[20] This did anger the colonels but was not discussed further.

Most of the men had returned home by summer, but our regiment maintained enlistment and won much favor with Jackson. We engaged the Creeks and established their hostility or appeasement and reported to Carroll. Many Creeks wanted our favor and reported British bribes to them. In September it was reported that Washington City had fallen, and Madison was in hiding.[21] They had then moved south and burned Baltimore. Jackson had gone to Mobile.

---

19 Sam Houston later became governor of Tennessee and the father of Texas.

20 William Weatherford held a formal parlay and surrendered to General Jackson after the Battle of Horseshoe Bend.

21 On August 24, 1815, British forces captured and burned the capital city.

The Brits were cavorting with the Creeks in Pensacola and had plans to move more soldiers north. Furthermore, the Spanish were having their way with the coast. Jackson sent us to probe Pensacola. The Creeks, now called Seminoles, were attacking outlying settlements and farms, using the arms from the British inciters. The Spanish were exacting defiance upon us by tolerating the British and Seminoles.

In November, Jackson, with much hesitation, took Pensacola with little issue. It was now understood the British were to take New Orleans. Jackson had both hatred and affinity for Indians and viewed many chiefs with admiration, though no fire in hell matched Jackson's vile disgust of the British and the king. Jackson moved all efforts toward New Orleans. He declared the entire city under his direction, and a titan effort of fortifying was begun.[22]

Our regiment was to continue our moonlight operations. We probed and dispatched their sentries nightly, while daytime was spent digging and fortifying. The night before Christmas saw an especially large and organized assault against the British. Many were killed and taken. This continued for a week.

The Tennesseans were moved to Chalmette under Carroll, and a great effort was made for ample trenches

---

22 On December 16, 1814, martial law was imposed on the city of New Orleans.

and breastworks.[23] On the morning of January 8, the British attacked en masse. God's almighty hand was with us. The British had no fear of our rifles, and a cruel scene of death was revealed unlike any seen before. They made more attempts over the next days, but the lines held. All British commanders had been killed. We were soon exchanging prisoners as the British continued to retreat.

Many spoils and gold for bribes had been taken from the officers. This bounty was guarded near the McCarty house.[24] At this time, an agent of the Baratarians[25] who had accompanied Lafitte was discovered to have left in the night on horse-back, loaded with all he could carry of the British gold. I was ordered to the McCarty house. When I arrived, Jackson and Laffite were there. Jackson had informed me that a Mr. Deveraux had made haste with the spoils that belonged to Mr. Laffite. He then told Laffite that I was a trusted emissary and had served well for him. He asked that I pursue Deveraux and kill him on sight and return the property to Mr. Laffite. The gold was in Spanish coinage. I left without delay.

---

23 The eastern line of Jackson's army at the Battle of New Orleans was the Chalmette plantation and was manned by the Tennessee Militia.

24 The McCarty house was a structure north of the American line in New Orleans and was used as Jackson's headquarters.

25 This refers to the band of "privateers" who came with Jean Laffite to help defend New Orleans against the British.

It was discovered that Deveraux was moving north. I and two corporals gave chase. Two days later we learned he had passed through a Dutch village and had left a few hours before. In the large prairie north of there, we saw him on horseback. We rode and dispatched him and brought his body and the two bags of Spanish gold he had taken. The man and the gold were returned to Laffite in New Orleans three days later.

Our regiment continued to monitor the Brits as they embarked. By March the British had gone, and the General released the city. I returned home the next week.

—Captain Barbee Collins
First Regiment, West Tennessee Volunteers, Metcalf Brigade

CHAPTER 10

THE PURSUIT

———◆———

WYATT WAS ALMOST TWENTY-ONE YEARS old, and Maggie, almost twenty. He sat on the couch in the trailer house in Flintville. Maggie was sitting in a chair across from him, trying to read and calm herself but with no success. A few hours earlier, a man had given them a check for one million dollars. They had gone through all the stages of emotion after returning from depositing the check. They had screamed and cried and then danced around and then leaped into the air like lunatics.

Now they had calmed enough to at least sit, but they did not know what to do next. They could not even decide what to think about as too many thoughts and possibilities flooded their attempts. Life had thrown them a sudden joker that now allowed them to go in any direction they wanted. They could buy a house. They could buy a car. They could go anywhere in the world they wanted, and Wyatt thought they probably would. But for now, he sat with his mind racing.

The fall sun was shining its warm orange light through the windows of the trailer they rented. It was October, and the night was pleasant. The air conditioner was off, and bird chirps from outside could be heard. Wyatt stared blankly at the wall and picked at his fingernails. His thoughts jumped from one vision to another. He thought of all the temporary difficulties that had been instantaneously solved. Wyatt also reflected back on his past. He mused over the times his life had changed profoundly and thought about episodes in his past that had changed the chapters of his life without warning. When he was seven, he felt that his world was stable, but in an instant it had changed to a completely different form. His father's death created at totally new existence for those he left behind, one no longer separated from a town. Likewise, when he obtained his driver's license and bought the green pickup truck, his life had changed again. Now a new chapter had begun, completely by surprise, when Marcel Dupree gave him a million dollars for the three gold coins they had found.

This also made him think of his debt to Maggie. It was Maggie who had pushed him to take her back to the mill to look under the rock. He would never have given another thought about looking if it had not been for her. Furthermore, a new chapter had just opened for Maggie as well. Wyatt had noticed some recent changes in her, but more changes were inevitably coming. She was already much different from the awkward, standoffish girl she had been in when he met her. Wyatt could tell she had changed even since they had worked at the petting zoo. She had proved to be more helpful and resourceful than he guessed she would be. She was wearing dresses now. She fussed with her hair. She put on makeup, usually. She also talked differently by standing up straighter and speaking more articulately. Wyatt had once thought she was okay looking. Now he thought she was pretty.

His appearance had also changed drastically over this time span as well. Maggie now thought he was handsome. Maggie had learned how to flirt and was unashamed to as she had settled into loving Wyatt, who liked it and flirted back in return. They were intimate more often. She readily surrendered to his judgment and depended on Wyatt willingly. She gave him full support and loyalty and was efficient at making a little go a long way. Wyatt was also steadfastly prudent with his money and not wasteful, which helped Maggie feel secure about depending on him.

"What are you going to do, Wyatt? What are you thinking about?" asked Maggie. She could not stand the silence.

"Heck, I don't know. We could do anything, I guess," said Wyatt.

"What do you want to do?"

"I don't even know. What do you want to do?"

"I don't want to have to decide yet," said Maggie.

"No, I don't guess we have to." Wyatt paused for a moment. "We should buy a house. Don't you think we should look for a house?"

"Where would you want to live?"

"I have no idea. I have not looked around enough yet. Maybe we should get a mobile home."

"I don't know. A real house might be better," said Maggie.

"I'm going to trade in the pickup. I want us to be able to go anywhere. I'm going to trade it in for a bigger one! What about that?"

"When?"

"Heck, I don't know. You want to go tomorrow?"

"Sure, I'll go with you. Where will we go once we have this new truck?"

"We will go everywhere. Where do you want to go? Shoot, we could get one of those big nice campers to go on the back. We could go anywhere in that."

"Yes, I guess we could," she said.

"I guess I just want to pack up and go for a while. Let's trade the truck in and just go. It won't matter how far or where."

"I like that idea," said Maggie. "Maybe on the road, we will figure out what we want to do.

"That sounds like a good plan for now," he said. "We will go get a new rig tomorrow."

The next day, instead of complicating their lives by buying things, they simplified their lives. They traded in the green pickup for a used Dodge Ram diesel. It was a four-wheel drive, four-door crew cab, with a full eight-foot bed, in silver. When they drove it off the lot, they drove to a camper store in Fayetteville and got the "Silver Beast" fitted with an over-the-cab camper that would carry their entire collection of worldly belongings for the foreseeable future. They were both giddy with excitement.

Wyatt called the landlord to tell him this month would be their last at the trailer and thanked him. Wyatt also called

Mr. MacAnally and told him what had happened and that he would be moving on, and Wyatt thanked him for his kindness and generosity. Wyatt settled his affairs, paid off the dentist, and could now leave Flintville. Wyatt and Maggie were free on the earth.

When they left Flintville in the Silver Beast, they still had not decided which way they would go. They left the trailer home knowing they would not likely be back, and neither of them needed to say good-bye to it. When they turned out of the driveway, Wyatt decided that if nothing else, he would drive to Illinois and tell his sister Cora what had happened. Plus, he had not seen her since leaving Layton, though they had spoken on the phone.

Cora and Lawrence lived in Buncombe, Illinois. Lawrence had started a small construction business there, and he and Cora were doing well. When Wyatt and Maggie began, they headed northwest around Nashville and then north again through Land between the Lakes. The winding road between Lake Barkley and Kentucky Lake was manicured on both sides, and the brown forest was sparse, having lost all of its leaves. Squirrels, chipmunks, and deer scurried in the road and out of their way as they passed. Wyatt called Cora and told her where they were and that they would be coming to see her. He apologized for the short notice. Cora was excited. She begged Wyatt to plan to stay the night when they got there, and she would fix a big supper. By evening they had arrived.

When Wyatt pulled the Silver Beast into the driveway, Cora came out onto the porch. Cora was in shock at the size of the truck and huge camper she saw, after expecting his green pickup. She also did not expect his pomaded hair and new, sharper look.

"Wyatt! You don't even look the same," said Cora. She ran to him and began to cry. "You look good. I'm so happy to see you." She hugged him again and dabbed at her tears. "Where did you get that truck? What happened to your green one?"

"It is a long story, but I came to tell you about it. You won't believe it!" said Wyatt.

"I can't wait to hear it," she said and hugged him. I've made a big supper, and Lawrence will be here soon."

"Cora, this is Maggie," said Wyatt. Cora walked to Maggie and hugged and welcomed her.

"Hello, Cora," said Maggie. "It is really nice to finally meet you."

Cora was pleased by Maggie's prettiness and pleasantness. Cora showed them into the house.

Wyatt and Maggie sat at the kitchen table while Cora finished the meal she had prepared. Wyatt told her about some of the minor adventures they had been on, but he avoided the coins for now. Wyatt was glad to be with Cora and was also glad to see her happy. About an hour later, Lawrence came home.

Lawrence had grown a little rounder and balder since Wyatt had seen him last. He had curly reddish hair that stuck out on the sides and was thin on top. He cheeks were plump and red. Cora met him at the door as Lawrence entered the house to tell him her brother was there.

"Wyatt! It is good to see you!" said Lawrence. "How have you been?"

"Doing great. You?" said Wyatt.

"Staying busy, man. Staying busy. Is that your silver rig out there?"

"Sure is."

"Dang, son! That is sharp. What happened to the green one?"

"Well, that is one of the things I came to tell you about."

"Well, I can't wait to hear about that!" said Lawrence.

Cora announced that supper was ready and pulled a roast from the oven, along with potatoes and carrots with fresh bread. Cora was a great cook. They all sat down and began eating.

"Well, now, Wyatt, what is this 'thing' you wanted to tell us?" asked Cora.

"I guess it's time," said Wyatt, "but some of it will be difficult to believe at first."

"What is it, Wyatt?" pressed Cora.

"You remember a few months ago when we went and saw two of our uncles? Luke and Charlie?"

"Yes," said Cora.

"Well, Luke had some old junk of one of our great-great-grandpappy's and gave it to us. It was an old busted clock and a journal. It turns out no one had been able to read the journal for eons because it was all stuck together. Well, out of curiosity, Maggie steamed the pages apart, and we were able to read the letter. This took a few weeks, mind you."

Cora and Lawrence stared at Wyatt and waited for the point of the story.

"Then," Wyatt continued, "We found a letter in the clock written by or to the same grandpappy, who mentioned a secret something hidden under a rock at an old mill. Believe it or not, when we went to New Orleans, we found the location of the mill."

"You two just drove around and found it?" asked Cora. Maggie was quiet as usual but nodded to Cora.

"Yep, but it gets better," said Wyatt. "When we found it, it was covered in junk and debris, so we left. But we went back two weeks later and dug under a big rock and found three coins, just like the letter said, except the letter called it soap."

"Soap?" asked Cora confused.

"Three gold coins?" said Lawrence. "Three gold coins won't pay for a truck like that."

"You are right," said Wyatt. "We took the coins and tried to sell them, only to find out they were minted for the king of Spain three hundred years ago, and only a handful of them were made. We had to take them to Atlanta."

"Atlanta," said Lawrence becoming increasingly intrigued by the progress of Wyatt's tale.

"Yes, we took them to an antiquities dealer, who said they had become quite valuable while sitting there in the hole under the rock. He bought them from us." Wyatt stopped and looked at Cora and Lawrence.

Lawrence's mouth was hanging open.

"He bought them from you?" asked Cora.

"Yep," said Wyatt.

"For how much?" she asked.

"Are you ready?"

"Yes, yes, tell me!" said Cora.

"One million dollars," said Wyatt.

There was silence. Cora and Lawrence just looked at Wyatt and Maggie.

"A million dollars?" asked Cora, now looking at Maggie.

"Yes, that is right," said Maggie.

"You mean to tell me you found three coins and sold them for a million dollars, and that is how you got the truck?" asked Lawrence.

"I told you it would be hard to believe," said Wyatt.

"You got a million dollars for them?" asked Cora again, to make sure what she was hearing was real. "This is no joke, Wyatt?"

"No joke," said Wyatt.

"No shit! A million dollars," said Lawrence.

"No shitting," said Wyatt.

"You are set for a while."

"I think so."

"Did you pay the taxes yet?"

"No, that is something I will have to look into soon," said Wyatt.

"Yep," said Lawrence. "What are you going to do with it?"

"Probably buy a house someplace eventually and maybe start a business, but that may be a while."

"A million dollars," Lawrence repeated.

The mood was light as they sat in their living room. They joked about going places and seeing people. Cora talked about exotic, beautiful places she would go. Wyatt liked seeing her happy and dreaming. After a while it was getting late, and Lawrence went to bed, leaving Wyatt, Maggie, and Cora in the living room.

"Have you talked to Mom? Will she talk on a phone?" asked Wyatt.

"Yes, every once in a while. She is doing well, about the same. She doesn't seem to know what's going on much, but she doesn't seem to be bothered by anything. She just stays there with Justine."

"How is Justine?"

"Feeble," said Cora.

"Does Mom ask about me?"

"She doesn't really ask about anything, but I tell her about you."

"What do you tell her about me?" he asked.

"That you are out working in wheat fields and mowing yards, and that you have a girlfriend."

"What does she say?"

"Nothing. She just smiles."

"Over the phone," he laughed.

"Yes, she is not really good with a phone, not ever really having one until Justine's. She even calls it 'Justine's phone,'" said Cora, giggling.

"Do you think I should go there?"

"You could, but she won't be mad if you don't."

"Why is she that way, Cora?"

"I don't know. I guess it is because her parents were kind of slow and quiet. And she has always depended on someone."

"Who is she dependent upon now?"

"Social Security now. But in her mind, it is Daddy," said Cora.

"I see," Wyatt said. They sat quietly for a moment and let sleepiness embrace them.

"This all seems surreal, Wyatt. You getting that money and all," said Cora. She turned to Maggie and added, "Of all things."

"I know. I can't believe it either," said Maggie.

"Life is crazy," said Cora.

"It sure is," said Wyatt.

Tears formed in Cora's eye. "It was the worst on you when Daddy died, Wyatt. You were so young, and things changed so fast."

"I know, but I'm doing okay."

"I'm sorry about all that, but I'm glad this happened to you, Wyatt. You deserve it."

"Thank you, Cora."

They went to bed soon after that.

The next morning, the family woke early. Cora fixed a breakfast while she and Maggie sat talking at the table. Lawrence had gone outside and was leaving for work but was looking at Wyatt and Maggie's Silver Beast.

"Where do you think you will go first?" asked Lawrence.

"I'm guessing we will head west," said Wyatt.

"Any place in particular?"

"No, not yet. We may find a couple of places to hang out for the winter."

"Sounds good, man. You two be safe. It was good to see you."

"You too. Take care of Cora."

"I will."

They shook hands, and Lawrence left.

Wyatt walked back inside to say his good-byes to Cora. The good-bye was tearful for Cora. She was happy for Wyatt, and she wished him well as she hugged him repeatedly before he and Maggie left.

When Wyatt and Maggie left Buncombe they went north for no particular reason. Since they had no idea where they wanted to go, Wyatt decided to head everywhere by making a big circle. Wyatt was slightly curious as to what the wheat country in Montana looked like in the winter. For now, they would begin the great loop at the top. If something came along that interrupted the loop, it would be okay with them.

They bypassed St. Louis by staying to the east and then passed Milwaukee by staying to the west. They spent the night in Madison, Wisconsin. They veered west around the Great Lakes and passed Minneapolis and came to Fargo, North Dakota. Maggie suggested they go north from Fargo into Canada to Winnipeg and then travel west on the road from Winnipeg to Calgary. The Canadian border was not diffi-cult. A young, firm-faced Canadian border officer looked at their identification and peeked into the camper before waving them past. They stayed the night in Winnipeg.

The hours on the road so far had not cultivated any decisions about their lives, or what they should do next. They did not even speak much. Maggie found stations on the Beast's fancy radio, and she even called the number and activated XM radio. The music played while they ruminated their future. Wyatt thought about the money. He knew nearly half of it would go to taxes, and the price of a house would take a huge chunk of the remainder. He thought about Cora and wanted to be able to help her if she ever needed it.

The next morning they got up and wanted to make it to Calgary by day's end. The frozen lakes and frosted evergreen forests were beautiful along the road as it went through old trapping towns with Indian or animal names. They soon found their clothes were not sufficient for this colder country. When they stopped to get fuel, the cold air stung their faces, ears, and lungs. When evening approached, they were coming into Calgary. They stopped at a Salvation Army Store, and both of them got more layers and heavy parkas with hoods. They stayed the night in Calgary.

The next morning in the motel lobby, they looked at a map and brochure for nearby Banff National Park. "Plenty of winter campsites available," caught their attention, and they thought it worth their while to check it out.

The park was made up of frozen streams and tall, snow-covered evergreens. The narrow road through the forest was lined with piles of snow from the scraping trucks on either side. They continued around the icy curves until they came to the campground, which surrounded a large lodge in the center. There were only two open spots available, and Wyatt pulled the Silver Beast into one of them and got out to plug the camper in to the electric box. It was bitterly cold, and every step of the process was painful.

"Wyatt, this is beautiful, but I'm afraid we are going to freeze to death," said Maggie.

"Yes, we are going to have to stay inside," said Wyatt. "I am freezing my balls off!"

They got into the back of the camper and began to set it up for a couple days' stay. After a while they had mustered up the nerve to bundle up and try to walk around outside. They put on every stitch of clothing they had that would provide warmth. They wrapped up their faces and pulled the hoods over their heads and climbed out of the camper and stood in the freezing wind.

"Let's walk over to the lodge and see what is going on in there," said Wyatt.

They walked up to the lodge door. On the heavy wooden door, a banner read, "Indigenous People of Canada Festival." They opened the door and went inside. Inside there were two dozen or so dark-haired, squinty-eyed people in colorful shirts and furry boots. Against one wall of the building were piles of parkas and coats. Two of the dark-haired men looked at them and waved in a welcoming way but did not reveal any additional emotions. The others did not seem to notice or mind their arrival. It was warm inside, and free coffee was available near the door. Maggie got them a cup and they sat down at a table near the fireplace that was warming the room. They watched as a group of the natives chatted with each other about what was on their minds, in languages Wyatt and Maggie could not understand. Wyatt thought they seemed to be talking about practical issues like power outages and shipment delays, but he could not be sure.

After a while they saw a man walk into the lodge. He was tall and thin. His long black hair was over his ears, and the skin around his dark thin eyes was worn and weathered. He was hatless. His thin jacket was unbuttoned two buttons down, and his bare chest was showing, but the man seemed unaffected by the miserable cold outside. He looked around the room through his large, ill-fitting glasses. He moved slowly toward them and eventually sat at the table where Maggie and Wyatt were sitting.

"Hello, and how are you two?" he said to them in the long vowels of an Eskimo accent.

"We are good, sir," said Wyatt. "How are you?"

"Oh, very good. What tribe are you with?"

"We are not with a tribe. We are from America, and we are just driving through," said Wyatt.

"Oh, I see. Well, welcome. This is the annual meeting for the 'frozen tribes,'" the man said as he smiled. "We talk about different tribal problems and try to find solutions."

"Are you from here?" asked Wyatt.

"No," he said. "I'm the mayor of Old Crow, Yukon. That is more than a thousand miles from here to the north."

"A thousand miles north? I bet that is cold!"

"Yes."

"My name is Wyatt, and this is Maggie. What is your name?"

"My name is Alex Kyskavichik."

"It is nice to meet you, Alex."

"Same to you. Are you going to be here for the music tonight?" asked Alex.

"Maybe so. Who is playing?"

"Me," said Alex. "I am a Gwitch'in fiddler."

"Oh wow! What is a Gwitch'in?"

"It is the name of our tribe. We got some of our culture from European trappers that settled there in Northern Canada, and some of us play the fiddle. We dance too."

"That sounds fascinating. We will try to make it."

"Great, it will be in about three hours. See you then." Alex stood and nodded good-bye and walked over to a man he recognized to talk to him about some issue that was on his mind.

Wyatt and Maggie sat in the warmth of the lodge awhile longer before wrapping up again to go back outside. In the frigid wind, they found the deposit box for camping fees. Wyatt's fingers ached as he put the dollars into the envelope before dropping it into the slot in the metal box. Afterward, they walked quickly back to the camper and got in. Wyatt lay on the spacious and soft camper bed that hung out over the cab. Maggie collected a few things to eat and made more coffee for warmth. The time passed quickly, and soon it was time to bundle up for the return journey to the lodge to hear Alex the Gwitch'in fiddler.

When they walked in, Alex was sitting on the side of the hearth in front of the fireplace. He had on snowshoes and was tuning a fiddle. The other men and women were gathering chairs around the fireplace to hear him play. Someone turned off the overhead lights, leaving only the light of the fire. Alex looked up and smiled at everyone when the lights went off. With no introduction, he began playing tunes. The orange glow of the fire illuminated half of Alex's squinting face as he played scratchy fiddle tunes in the eerie light. He tapped the wooden snowshoes against the hardwood floor as the played. The dark faces watching and listening to Alex were silent as they listened with their eyes closed.

"What a strange spectacle," Wyatt thought. He and Maggie sat and enjoyed the surreal performance in the dark, warm lodge. Wyatt figured this was how Alex must play his tunes at home wherever he lived, huddled around a fire in the dark. He played fifteen or so tunes. Some were fast, and some were slow and mournful. When Alex finished, everyone applauded, and he put away his fiddle. The lights came back on, and he took off his snowshoes without saying anything. The rest of the listeners began to stand and mill around, grabbing their coats. Wyatt and Maggie were last in line to exit when Alex approached them with his fiddle case in hand.

"Did you like it?" asked Alex.

"Yes, we did," said Wyatt.

Alex, Wyatt, and Maggie began putting on their coats and layers in order to head back to the camper. Wyatt noticed that Alex's coat was ridiculously thin, and he did not wear a hat or a hood.

"I will walk out with you. I think we are camped together," said Alex.

The three of them walked out of the lodge together and moved toward the camper. Wyatt had not paid much attention to the small orange tent set up near them. It was partially covered with a drift of snow. As they neared the Silver Beast, Alex spoke up.

"Well, there is my tent, you have a warm night."

"Tent? That is your tent?" asked Wyatt.

"Yes," said Alex.

"How do you not freeze?"

Alex laughed and said, "Gwitch'ins don't freeze," as he got into his tent and zipped it behind him.

The next morning Wyatt and Maggie were planning to head south away from the arctic wind when they walked into the lodge. There sat Alex. He seemed bright-eyed and well rested as he wore only a thin button-up cotton shirt under his ever unbuttoned jacket. They got some coffee and sat down next to Alex at the table where he was sitting.

"How are you this morning, Alex?" asked Wyatt.

"Doing okay," he said. "I've got a bit of a problem this morning."

"What is it?" asked Wyatt.

"When I came down here, I caught a ride but all I had was my backpack. Going back I need to take two big boxes of circuit breakers for a big diesel generator. I have to take them with me, and they are going to take up a lot of room."

"What are you going to do?"

"I don't know yet." After a pause, Alex continued. "Are you going north in your big camper?"

"No, sir. We weren't planning on it."

"Oh, that is too bad. You should. I'll ride with you."

"To the Yukon?" asked Wyatt.

"Well, most of the way. You can't drive all the way there this time of year. They will send a plane for me in Carmacks."

Wyatt considered it. He turned to Maggie. "Maggie, what do you think about driving Mr. Alex north?"

"Will it be cold?" she asked.

"Yes," said Alex.

This worried Maggie that it would be so cold that even Alex thought it would be cold.

"The town of Old Crow will reimburse you for the trip," Alex said.

Wyatt didn't really need the money, but Alex's offer of reimbursement did sweeten the deal. Wyatt knew Maggie did not care for the cold and figured she had some reservations. He looked at her. He could tell she was not sure she was going to enjoy all of what was to come, but she was not the type to turn down an adventure. Maggie gave no audible objections. He figured the truck would do well and he was curious what "up north" was like. Other than it being cold he couldn't think of a reason not to go.

"I guess we can," said Wyatt.

"Oh, good. That solves a bunch of problems. When can we leave?"

Wyatt instantly regretted accepting.

"Whenever you want," he said.

"I will pack," said Alex.

Instead of heading south, Wyatt and Maggie found themselves heading further north into the arctic unknown with a Yukon Gwitch'in mayoral fiddler in the seat behind them. Alex was good with directions and pointed them north through Edmonton and beyond. Wyatt and Maggie found Alex to be pleasant. He rarely made a sound during the drive, and they were entertained by his eccentricities. Earlier in the day they saw him sleeping while sitting straight up with his eyes open. They were about an hour north of Calgary when Maggie resumed *Don Quixote* on Wyatt's phone. They were laughing at Quixote and Sancho's adventure in an enchanted boat, and them being called "foolish as jackasses." Maggie and Wyatt laughed when they realized then also were foolish as jackasses for agreeing to go on this journey, although they were enjoying it so far. Wyatt looked into the rearview mirror to see if Alex was finding any humor in the story. Instead, he saw Alex sitting there stone-faced and sitting perfectly still. After a second or two, Wyatt noticed Alex's gaze was glassy and he seemed to be in a daze. Wyatt reached over and touched Maggie's hand to get her attention silently. She noticed Wyatt and he gestured toward the back seat. Maggie looked at Alex and studied him in his trance for a moment."

"I think he is asleep," she whispered to Wyatt.

"With is eyes open?"

"That is pretty weird," she said.

"Yep," Wyatt replied.

Alex stayed in this state for several more minutes. A pump in the road eventually disturbed his slumber, and he awoke to see Wyatt looking at him in the rearview mirror.

"Where you asleep, Alex?" asked Wyatt.

"Sure was," said Alex.

"You sleep with your eyes open," said Wyatt.

Alex smiled, "My mother says I have done that since a child."

"It's a pretty cool trick," said Wyatt jokingly.

"Yes, I have always been 'the odd one'," said Alex. "That is what they called me in school. Of course, there was only six of us and two of them my brothers."

This made Wyatt and Maggie laugh. Maggie said, "Well, they must like you now since you are the mayor."

"That is a funny story too," said Alex. "I am mayor quite accidentally. I used to fetch things for the city council, and once when I was gone for a few days going after a fuel pump for a road grater, the mayor got mad and quit. Then the council met and couldn't get anyone to agree to be mayor, so they appointed me because I was not there to object. When I returned, they told me about it but it was too late, they already filled out the papers."

This made Wyatt and Maggie laugh again and the response brought a faint smile to Alex's usually expressionless face. The exchange brought out some of Alex's curiosity as well.

"What is you two do at home?" asked Alex. Wyatt nor Maggie knew how to answer his question.

"Well, that is hard to say," said Wyatt, "we are just driving around for a while. We are from Tennessee and we recently sold some coins we found. Now, we can't decide what to do next."

"What an adventure," said Alex. "Those coins must have been valuable."

"They were. We did not know it at first. We were taken by surprise when we were offered a million dollars for them. But, we took the money, and that was a week ago."

"You've been a millionaire for a week?"

"Yes," said Wyatt.

Alex contemplated this is silence for a while before continuing. "So when you became a millionaire last week, the first thing you decided to do was to drive into the Canadian tundra?" Alex asked jokingly but with no expression.

As their days drive came to its end, fewer and fewer green things poked up above the snow, and the endless blanket of white overtook the land in all directions. In the small town of Fort Nelson, Alex knew a man who had a shop where they could plug in the camper, and the three of them slept in the camper until they resumed their journey the next morning.

The next day's drive from Fort Nelson to Carmacks was exhausting. The icy road was shared with semis and equipment trucks making their way to and from the isolated towns.

Frequently the road was not wide enough for the big truck and the Silver Beast, thus requiring tender maneuvering. The sun blinded Wyatt as it reflected off the ubiquitous snow and ice through the glass of the windshield. The road, being mostly scraped ice, was slick as could be. The Beast slid and drifted left and right as it struggled for traction in the stiff wind. As it grew dark, they arrived in Carmacks.

It was hardly a town at all. It was a series of buildings between a gray road and a flat icefield that served as a runway for the small planes that served the area. Alex directed them toward one of the buildings and showed Wyatt where he could plug in the camper.

"A plane will be here in the morning. This worked out nicely," said Alex.

"I'm glad," said Wyatt.

"What do you think of this country so far?" asked Alex.

"It is beautiful," said Wyatt, "but the cold would take some getting used to."

"I suppose so," said Alex. "Why don't you come to Old Crow with me?"

"Come with you? In the plane?" asked Wyatt.

"Yes, I have to come back in three days. You can stay with me until then."

"Man, I don't know," said Wyatt.

"The town will pay for your fuel back if you take me back with you," said Alex, hoping to convince them.

"I guess we could. Do you think we will freeze?"

"No, you will be fine. It will be warm in the cabin."

Wyatt looked at Maggie. She shrugged, indicating her approval if Wyatt wanted to.

"Well, I guess we can," said Wyatt.

"Good," said Alex. He then lay down on the small lower bed in the camper and closed his eyes. Wyatt and Maggie sat looking at each other in silence. Their eyes indicated excitement at such an adventure, but they both knew the dreaded cold would be intense. The next morning they got up and brought the boxes of breakers into the hanger. Before long, a yellow single-engine plane landed and pulled up next to the hanger.

"There he is," said Alex. Alex walked out and greeted the pilot as he got out of the plane. They walked to the back of the plane and began making room for the boxes and two additional passengers. When they were done, Alex waved for Wyatt and Maggie to come over. The three of them, plus the pilot, got into the plane. Wyatt and Maggie brought all of their layers with them for the cold ahead. The plane took off, and soon they were looking down at the sea of white. Only a few random shacks with smoke coming out of them or the occasional caribou herd could be seen for the three-hour trip.

Soon they touched down in Old Crow, Yukon. They climbed out of the airplane onto the subarctic plain. They wrapped their faces and shielded their eyes, as it was bitterly cold. Alex walked toward a shed through the wind with his head still uncovered and his jacket unbuttoned. A few minutes later, they heard a motor start in the shed where Alex had gone. They saw a snowmobile come out. Alex drove the snowmobile behind the shed and hooked it to a sled. He drove the snowmobile and sled over to the yellow plane.

"This is our ride," he said as he turned off the motor and dismounted. Alex then put the two big boxes of circuit breakers from the plane onto the sled behind the snowmobile.

"Are you ready?" asked Alex.

"We just ride behind you?" asked Wyatt.

"Yes, it is about fifteen miles away. We are almost there."

Maggie and Wyatt had no other choice than to get on the snowmobile behind Alex. The cold wind was nearly unbearable when the snowmobile got up to speed toward Alex's cabin. Even Alex put on goggles and finally buttoned his jacket. Wyatt and Maggie both pulled their legs up close to their bodies and squeezed their hooded heads farther into their coats and sheltered themselves from as much wind as they could behind Alex's body. After about forty-five minutes, they arrived at Alex's cabin. They could still move their fingers and toes, but they were in pain from the cold. The cabin was a small three-room structure heated by a fire that was not lit when they got inside.

"It will be warm in here soon," said Alex, and he lit the wood already stacked into the metal stove. Alex showed them a corner of the room covered in caribou fur where Wyatt and Maggie could stay. Once they got settled, they put on some furry parkas Alex had as well as some arctic goggles, and they tried going outside again. They fared a little better this time, being more fortified against the cold air. Nonetheless, this only lasted a few minutes, as any exertion caused stinging of the lungs. The two of them ventured outside only for brief moments two other times, as the cold was too piercing. Alex was a gracious host and kept the cabin comfortable for them. He fed them dried salmon and boiled caribou meat in addition to oatmeal mush. Alex also played the fiddle for them around the firelight from the woodstove at night. All sorts of locals came to speak with Alex, but the conversations were held in the native Gwitch'in language, so they could not tell what was being said. But they could tell Alex was a beloved member of this tundra community. Wyatt and Maggie grew slightly bored and restless in the cabin after a couple of days but were still enjoying their spontaneous adventure with Alex.

After three days, they were back on the yellow plane as it took them back to Carmacks and the Silver Beast. Upon arrival, they loaded into the Beast. It was slow to crank due to the cold but after a couple of tries the motor cranked, and they headed back south. Once on the road, Alex gave Wyatt $800 in cash.

"Will this cover your fuel?" asked Alex.

"Yes," said Wyatt, "and thank you for asking us to bring you."

Alex smiled and said, "I can't believe you said 'yes.'" They spent the night again at Fort Nelson. The next day Alex had them drop him off at an acquaintance's business in Edmonton. Alex said he had a few more winter chores to settle. Alex did not say much when they departed, but he thanked them again and was gone with only a backpack and a thin shirt and jacket. It was December. Wyatt and Maggie headed south in the Silver Beast. They spent another night in Calgary but headed back across the border the next day.

When they crossed back into Montana, they had had enough of the cold. They crossed the border at Sweet Grass and went south through Great Falls. They stayed the night in Helena and continued south the next day. By the time they got to Salt Lake City, it was somewhat warmer, but the scenery was just as stark as it had been as they looked out the windows of the little yellow plane. They spent the night in the camper near a salt flat outside of the city before continuing south. At Saint George, before getting to Las Vegas, they took the small road toward Grand Canyon National Park.

The moment Wyatt first saw the canyon in the distance, he got the feeling and excitement of discovery, the sense of having found something. The beauty and spectacle of the Grand Canyon at least temporarily satisfied his longing to find something wonderful. Finding the coins had turned out to be spectacular but not immediately so. The colors and immensity of the gorges he saw now overwhelmed his imagination in real time. Maggie, like Wyatt, was in complete awe of what she saw out the window as they drove. There were miles and miles of deep gashes in the earth. Rocks of red and orange looked otherworldly. Small green evergreens grew from crevices in the rocks. All of this was lightly dusted with snow that was carried by the wind.

Most of the North Rim of the Grand Canyon was closed for the winter, so they went toward the South Rim and Lake Meade. The first night, they pulled into a camping spot only for an overnight stay, and they left the next morning to drive around and see more of the sights. On the afternoon of their second day, Wyatt had turned the Beast onto a small road around the edge of a red stone canyon. The area was flat on top, with a few large evergreen trees. As they drove farther, the area of land widened. A handful of camper sites fit onto the plateau, and they noticed a large camping rig packing up and leaving a spot under a few trees that overlooked a section of the gorge. When the big rig left, Wyatt took the spot with the Beast. Maggie and Wyatt got out and walked around.

"The air smells so clear," said Maggie.

"Yes, it is beautiful," said Wyatt.

They walked along the edge and looked into the gorge to see the brown water of the river barely visible below them. A red-tailed hawk was being harassed by smaller birds in the air far above the river but was still below the precipice where they were standing. Several trails to beautiful outlooks were within sight of the camper. The air was cool, but compared to where they had just been, it was pleasant. Wyatt set a folding chair from the camper on the ground and in only a light jacket closed his eyes and turned his face to the warm sun. This was a paradise.

They camped at this place for a week, taking hikes and exploring views around the South Rim. They found other places they would like to stay when they left their current location. One evening after they had been camped for a week, they were sitting outside of the camper in the cool breeze, watching the sunset.

"Have you thought any more about what you might want to do with the money?" asked Maggie.

"No, not really," said Wyatt. "I should probably start a business or invest it, but I don't know what in or where. What do you want to do?"

"We could do this for a while. There is no rush." Maggie said this in solidarity with Wyatt's problem of infinite options rather than in want of a gypsy's lifestyle. However, she was happy on the trip and wanted it to continue at least for a while.

"No, I guess not. I think the time will feel right when we find a place to settle. I haven't found it yet."

"Me neither," said Maggie, "but this place is close."

"Yes, I agree. I just want to see more."

"What kind of house do you think you will get?"

"Heck, I don't even know. Nothing too crazy. What kind would you like?"

Maggie did not say anything; rather, her eyes glistened with tears. She had reached a point at which she really did not care what kind of house she lived in. She would be happy with any home as long as Wyatt was there. Her love for him had solidified. She considered his happiness as much as she did her own. She was now fully committed to him. He had shown sacrifice and care for her. He now considered her comfort above his, and he had acknowledged her persistence as the reason they had found the coins. When she heard him talk about his future plans in the plural form and with consideration of her wishes, she only fell more deeply into his world, and his world brought her happiness.

"Tomorrow, do you think we might move to that other spot we saw?" she asked.

"Sure," said Wyatt. Wyatt looked at Maggie and smiled. He thought she looked beautiful in the evening dusk light, and he told her so.

"Thank you. I love you," she said. They went inside the camper and made love. Afterward, they lay there in exhaustion. Neither could have been happier. A few minutes later when their energy was restored, they had another round.

The next morning they moved the Beast a few miles down the small road to the other side of a series of gorges. The road went down in elevation onto a small piece of rocky ground with two walls of orange stone mountains on either side of them. They stayed at this spot for a week and enjoyed its cool nights and visiting critters until they moved on to another spot along a cove of Lake Meade. They continued this for three more weeks, staying at a spot until they found another. They drove into Flagstaff a few times for supplies and liked the town.

One evening they were sitting in chairs outside of the camper. They had just finished a hike and were snacking and getting ready for darkness to come when Wyatt received a phone call. Wyatt did not get many calls as he had not had a telephone for very long, and the calls he got were telemarketers. He wasn't on anyone's call list that he knew of, except for

Cora's. It was not Cora. It was from Atlanta. He picked it up and spoke.

"Hello?"

"Wyatt, how are you?" It was the French accent of Marcel Duprée.

"Marcel! I'm good. How are you?"

"Busy my friend, busy."

"That sounds good. What can I do for you?"

"Wyatt, I need you to do something for me," said Marcel. "I need to hire you for an event."

"Really?" Wyatt was shocked. "What is it, Marcel? What is the event?"

"The auction for your coins," said Marcel.

"Oh."

"The auction will be in two weeks. We have worked very hard to find a sale that would be appropriate for them," Marcel explained in his flowing way. "We found one. It will be in New York in two weeks."

"Wow, that sounds very exciting, Marcel. I'm glad it is working out for you, but why do you need me?"

"Well, things haven't worked out completely yet. The sale needs to be hyped, so to speak, to drive up the price. We have done that. We have put out ads, and there was a story in the *New York Times* about the coins, but I would like for you to be there also."

"But what would I do there?"

"It adds a human element of discovery. I need you there, Wyatt, to legitimize the find. I would like you to be there as their finder. People love treasure hunters. I want to sensationalize the coins. I want for people to ask you about how you found them and for you and Maggie to tell them the story of you digging them up. And the journal you used to find them. It will add to their legend. Can you come?"

"Well, I guess so," said Wyatt.

"I would really appreciate it. I will cover your expenses, and you can stay in the hotel there as a representative of European Antiquities."

"What hotel is it?"

"Ha ha! Trump Tower, if you can believe it! This sale will be at Trump Tower, so it will be easy to find."

"Well, okay, I guess."

"Excellent! Wyatt, this is super helpful. I will leave Atlanta in a week—one week before the sale. Call me when you get to town."

"Okay, I will."

"Thanks again," said Marcel.

Wyatt hung up.

Maggie was looking at him. "What was that about?" asked Maggie.

"It was Marcel. He wants us to come to New York when he sells the coins at auction. He wants us to be there as treasure hunters so people can ask us about the coins. He says he will pay our way. It is at Trump Tower."

"Wow, that's a surprise," said Maggie.

"Sure is."

"Trump Tower? Is that what he said?"

"Yep." He laughed when he said it.

"Are we going?" she asked.

"I guess so. Do you want to?"

"Sure. I've never been to New York."

"Me neither." Wyatt sat silently for a moment. He pondered the trip east and what New York and the East Coast would be like. He also considered what it would be like to have to answer questions about lost Spanish coins from wealthy antiquities buyers. It caused him some anxiety.

Maggie also was sitting quietly but was not still. She was fidgeting and shaking her leg with her foot. She looked troubled, and it was not the response Wyatt expected. Wyatt noticed her with the same countenance yesterday briefly. The idea of a New York trip seemed to have brought it out again.

"You don't want to go?" asked Wyatt.

"No, I'm fine with it."

"You seem bothered. What is it?"

"Wyatt, I think I am pregnant."

CHAPTER 11

NEW YORK

———————————

IT WAS THE END OF January when they left the Grand Canyon
for New York. Wyatt had received Maggie's announcement
well. She was nervous, as many newly pregnant women are.
Wyatt thought it best that he show only excitement about the
possibility. They drove through Flagstaff one last time and
stopped at a drugstore for a pregnancy test. It was positive. It
was official. The game had changed.

For the next few days, they did not talk about the future
and what it would bring in the next nine months because
there were too many variables. They did not even know
where they would be when the time came. Wyatt did realize
it would be up to him to find a place for Maggie and a baby.
The event at least gave him a timeline in the back of his mind
on which to build. Maggie becoming pregnant was like a star
in the night on which he could take a bearing.

They drove east along I-40. They stayed a night in
Albuquerque and then a night in Fort Smith, Arkansas. They
continued east and spent a night in Knoxville. They headed

north through the Appalachian Mountains. They drove through the beautiful Shenandoah Valley. Wyatt thought maybe in this picturesque countryside could be a small house with a few acres. He looked out the window in quiet thought as he drove along.

After a few days, Maggie was able to smile and talk about her situation. She smiled when Wyatt mentioned it and giggled as he talked about houses and schools. They had made good time and did not need to push hard to New York—until Marcel was there, anyway.

They drove to the outskirts of Washington, DC, and parked the Silver Beast in the lot of an end-of-the-line subway station, caught the subway, and rode into the city. The beautiful white monuments and buildings were impressive. They walked by the Capitol and by the Washington Monument. They went into a Smithsonian building and saw the trove of mounted animals, jewels, and gems it held. They got a hotel room, and the next day they were on foot again. To Wyatt the most noteworthy place in the city was the Jefferson building of the Library of Congress. Its ceiling of murals and carved walls and doors held racks and racks of the oldest books in the country. It was beautiful, and Wyatt could have stayed for days. However, they walked through more museums and stayed another night in the capital city.

The next day Wyatt called Marcel. Marcel suggested they hold on for two more days and meet him at Trump Tower on Friday. The sale was to be on Sunday evening.

When Friday came, they drove to an outlying subway station, parked the Beast as they had done in Washington, and got onto the train. The New York subway system took some getting used to. A couple of times they discovered they were on the wrong train, but they soon figured it out. The Fifty-Ninth and Columbus station was the subway stop closest to the tower. They emerged on foot from the subway stairs to see throngs of people. The station was on the corner of Central Park but was otherwise encircled by skyscrapers. It was Thursday when they arrived. Wyatt sent a message to Marcel saying they were in town and could meet him at Trump Tower. Marcel responded back to meet him "in the lobby bar at noon tomorrow." Wyatt and Maggie walked through Central Park until dark. They rode the subway back to the Beast and stayed the night in the camper.

The next morning they awoke, and Wyatt put on a cleaner pair of jeans and one of the button-up shirts Maggie had made for him. Maggie put on a blue dress and curled the ends of her hair. They got onto the subway and headed for the Fifty-Ninth Street station. It was about nine thirty in the morning when they made it to the corner of Central Park with the top of Trump Tower in sight. They walked around to pass some time, and at a few minutes before noon, they walked into the tower.

Its lobby was expansive and full of people. The amber bulbs and gold embellishments put off a yellow light throughout the entire space. They saw the lobby bar and walked toward it. Sitting and drinking a red wine was the tall and graceful Marcel Duprée, dressed in a gray pinstripe suit.

"Marcel," said Wyatt. Marcel turned around and was glad to see Wyatt. He stood and shook his hand.

"Wyatt, thanks so much for coming. Have you enjoyed the city so far?"

"Yes," said Wyatt. "It is quite a sight."

"Yes, indeed," said Marcel, "there is no other city in the world like it."

"It is incredible," said Wyatt.

"Let us go upstairs. I will show you where we will be." Marcel led them to the elevator with golden doors and illuminated mirrors on the inside. He pressed the button for the fifteenth floor. When they got off the elevator, they saw more golden fixtures and marble floors and walls. Marcel continued down a series of halls into a ballroom that would hold two hundred people or so.

"Here it is," Marcel said. He showed them a glass case where the coins were to be displayed. The sale would also feature a small Roman statue as well as a newly found painting by a famous artist. "I would like for you to be near the coins during the viewing and just be pleasant and answer questions. Be charming. Can you do that?"

"Yes, I think so."

"Good. We will need to look our best. Buyers want a piece of a legend. They desire a swashbuckling story! Did you bring a tuxedo?"

"Tuxedo? Why no. I did not even bring a suit. Heck, I don't even own a suit," said Wyatt.

"Hmm, this will not do. But there is time. Let me call," said Marcel. He stepped over into the corner of the room and dialed a number on his phone. He spoke in French to a person on the other end for a few minutes before hanging up. "I spoke to a friend of mine who has a small formal wear shop nearby," he said. "I told him the problem and that you and Maggie would come to see him. He will take care of you. He will deliver a tuxedo to your room."

"Oh, okay. Um, where is our room?" asked Wyatt.

"I will show you," said Marcel. They followed Marcel back down the halls to a set of rooms reserved for the event stagers. "We have a few of these, and you two can use this one, 15301." Marcel gave them a key, and Wyatt opened the door. They walked inside to see more marble walls and golden furniture. It was by far the nicest room either of them had ever been in. A large poster bed was in the corner. A small golden chandelier hung over it. The toilet was golden. The curtains were even golden. In another corner of the room was a marble landing and a set of spiral stairs that led up to a bathroom and shower with two heads.

"Will this do?" asked Marcel, smiling.

"Yes," said Wyatt.

Maggie was walking around the room, soaking up the grandeur.

"Now, you need to go see Robert"—he pronounced it *Row Bear*—"at the boutique before too long so he can deliver your clothes to the room," said Marcel.

Wyatt thanked Marcel, and he and Maggie headed to find the address Marcel had given them. The shop was a few blocks away near the Japan Society Building on Second and East Forty-Seventh Street. After several minutes they found it. It was sort of a hidden shop with a simple sign that read, "Formal du Paris." When they walked in they saw many rows of dark and sleek suits, and on one row were several sparkling dresses drenched in sequins and lace. The owner came up to them.

"Hello. I am Robert. How may I help you?"

"Did Marcel call you?"

"Ah, yes. Are you the ones?"

"Yes," said Wyatt.

"Right this way," said Robert. He took a cloth tape measure from his pocket and began measuring Wyatt's shoulders, legs, and waist. He then walked over and pulled a black tuxedo jacket from a hanger and held it for Wyatt to put on. It fit perfectly. Wyatt looked into a large mirror. He looked sharp.

"You will need a tie. My dear, what color dress are you wearing?" Robert asked Maggie.

"I don't have one yet," she said.

"Oh, I see. We will fix that." He walked over to the wall of evening gowns. "Do either of these suit you? I believe either one should fit." He pointed to two dresses. One was purple and the other a champagne color with a sequined bodice and lace shoulders.

"That one is beautiful," she said pointing to the champagne dress.

"Yes, it is nice. Try it on, if you please," he said. He walked toward the dressing room and hung the dress on a hook inside. Maggie walked in and closed the curtain and began figuring out how to get the dress on. She figured it out and it fit. She had never felt more beautiful or glamorous than at that moment. In fact she had never felt glamorous before at all. Her eyes glistened with tears.

"Will this work?" asked Robert.

"Yes. Thank you," said Maggie.

"Excellent." I will get these ready and deliver them to your room tomorrow. This is going to be a great night for you two, I hope."

Wyatt and Maggie thanked him and walked back to the tower. That night their spirits were up, and they decided to walk through the city at night. They found the streets to be about as crowded at night as they were in the day, except that at night the people were in a party mood. The mood was contagious, and soon Wyatt and Maggie found themselves laughing arm in arm as they walked among the lights and tall buildings. By midnight they were partied out, and they went back to their room in Trump Tower.

The next morning they slept late but were awakened at about ten in the morning by a knock on the door. Wyatt answered it. At the door was a Trump Tower employee with two black bags on hooks.

"A delivery," said the porter. Wyatt thanked him and brought the clothes inside. Wyatt was unaware that a tip was appropriate. Wyatt hung them in a closet so they would be out of harm's way until the auction, which was the next day. They were getting hungry and decided to go to the lobby grill to grab a lunch. They got onto the elevator and took it to the lobby. When they got off, there were more people coming in and out than the day before in the lobby. In addition to the many people, there were two dozen reporters with cameras loitering around. They walked up to the lobby grill and Wyatt recognized the face of a man he had seen before, sitting at a table by himself. It was Fred, Marcel's lawyer.

"Fred," said Wyatt. Fred turned around.

"Wyatt, it is so good to see you." Fred gestured for them to sit at the table with him. "Marcel said he hoped you would come."

"So you are here for the sale as well?" asked Wyatt.

"Oh, yes. I prepare the paperwork to finalize the sale. It has been quite an ordeal scheduling an auction of this type. Marcel has worked himself ragged."

"Yes, indeed. It seems very involved," said Wyatt.

"It is, and it is not over yet. The auction must be well attended by wealthy collectors to make it work, but I think it will be."

"That is good," said Wyatt.

"What have you been doing since I saw you last—which was the day you became a millionaire, as I recall?"

Wyatt smiled. "We have been driving, mostly. We went to Canada, all the way to the Yukon."

"You don't say," said Fred. "In the winter?"

"Yes."

"Brave man," said Fred.

"Then we went to the Grand Canyon and stayed there for about six weeks until Marcel called."

"Well, you are a true adventurer, Wyatt. I'm envious."

"Thanks," said Wyatt.

"Maggie, you are a real trooper to follow Wyatt around like this," said Fred.

"It has been fun," said Maggie.

"Shoot. It is me following her," said Wyatt acknowledging her contributions. Maggie only smiled.

"Being a millionaire hasn't changed you much yet, I see, said Fred."

"I guess it hasn't. It sure doesn't seem much different. We still drive around and sleep in our pickup."

Fred laughed. "I bet it is a nice pickup, though."

"Indeed. The Silver Beast."

"Well done," said Fred. "Men in your family don't stay put for very long, it seems." Fred did not know much of Wyatt's history, but he was correct. "It seems you are descended from adventurers and doers."

"I don't know. I have not met many of them," said Wyatt.

"The man who buried those coins certainly was. He was a soldier, an officer who fought in multiple conflicts, apparently, and was a leader of men. He had no idea what he did for his descendants two hundred years ago. As a result, your life and the lives of your children will be different. It is phenomenal, really. I think that's why Marcel wanted you to be here, so the story of the coins would come into play."

"I don't know if Barbee Collins did it with his children in mind. I kind of thought he just never got a chance to go back. Heck, if he had gone back, there would be no story at all." Wyatt said this to Fred but looked at Maggie.

"I would say you have the same spirit as him. If only you could thank him for it," said Fred.

"Yes, if only," said Wyatt. Wyatt sat for a moment and thought of the continuum of time. This man—Barbee Collins, whom he knew little of—had indeed done him a great favor two centuries ago. Yet he had not intended to. The man who buried the coins gained nothing from them during his life, but due to the passage of time, Wyatt would benefit exponentially more.

"Marcel!" said Fred.

Wyatt's thoughts were interrupted by Fred seeing Marcel. He walked toward them and was visibly worried.

"What is the matter?" asked Fred.

"Damn it!" said Marcel. "He is here."

"Who?" said Fred.

"Trump," said Marcel.

"Oh, no," Fred said with a laugh. "That is going to complicate things."

"Yes, I know. This lobby will fill up, and people won't be able to get to the elevator. I was afraid this would happen."

"It may not be that bad," said Fred, trying to encourage Marcel.

"Maybe not. I just hope he doesn't pull any shenanigans." Marcel was aware of the attention Trump Tower had been getting because of its owner's political ambitions. Marcel was told that Mr. Trump would most likely be in Washington, DC, during the auction and would not impede events at the tower, but this had changed. Mr. Trump had come with no notice in the night and would be spending the weekend with the Japanese prime minister, Mr. Abe. This explained the increased number of people in the lobby this morning as well as the obvious security presence. Marcel hoped that Trump's presence would not have a negative effect on the auction by distracting the attendees.

"Wyatt, how did your visit go with Robert?" asked Marcel.

"Well, thank you. We are ready to go," said Wyatt.

"Excellent. Did you find a dress you liked?" he asked Maggie.

"Yes, thank you," she said.

Marcel told Fred that everything was in place, and there was not much else to do. The items to sell would be kept in the tower vault until tomorrow, when security would bring them to the displays in the ballroom on the fifteenth floor. He said that the auction would start at six o'clock, and they needed to be there by five to welcome the attendees and mingle. Wyatt told Marcel they understood.

Wyatt and Maggie spent the rest of the day at Central Park. The wind was cold, but the day was beautiful. The day passed quickly, and as night came, they walked through more of the city and joined in with the rest of the Saturday night revelers in their enjoyment of a New York City night. The next morning was the big day.

When they got up, Maggie got her borrowed dress out of its black hanging cover. Wyatt watched the television in the room as Maggie danced around the room and began to get ready. She climbed the stairs to the large bathroom and dressing room at the top. She showered and began fooling with her hair, which she did for an hour or more. She made several attempts at makeup, washing it off and starting over until she was satisfied. At about three o'clock, Maggie descended the stairs in a thin white slip. Wyatt had never seen her look so beautiful. Three weeks ago if someone had told Wyatt that he and Maggie would be in New York City wearing tuxedoes and gowns at a formal event in Trump Tower, he would not have believed it. Maggie had become fit and more tan since the start of their series of adventures. They were there to play the part of treasure hunters. Maggie looked the part.

"Wyatt, it is your turn. You need to shower and get ready. I will get out of your way and put on my dress while you shower," she said to Wyatt.

"Wowzer!" said Wyatt, looking at her as she passed him on the stairs. He tugged at her slip flirtingly as he went up the stairs. He showered quickly in the two-headed shower made to fill with steam. It was very nice. He inhaled the warm steam and closed his eyes. Maggie put on her ball gown while Wyatt finished. Feeling like a new man, Wyatt stepped out of the shower and toweled off and tied the towel around his waist. He looked in the mirror while he shaved and worked some pomade into his hair. He grabbed the folds of the towel, wrapped the towel around his waist like the handles of pistols, and breathed in deeply to observe himself. Looking into the mirror he felt like he looked pretty dang good himself, though maybe not as good as Maggie.

"Oh damn!" said Wyatt as he looked into the mirror.

"What? What is it?" asked Maggie.

"I am gooood-looking!"

"Oh please!" said Maggie with a giggle and an eye roll.

"Look away, Maggie. I don't know if you can handle this." Wyatt, now confident and cocky, refolded the towel around himself and started down the stairs with great pompous ceremony meant to entertain Maggie.

"What has gotten into you?" asked Maggie.

Wyatt put his foot onto the second step and replied, "I'm just really good-looking is all. Don't worry yourself."

No sooner had he delivered his cocksure comment than his wet foot slid on the marble step, and he fell. Maggie's first instinct was to laugh since his cockiness had backfired. He first landed on his back on the stairs, which caused him to hit his head quite hard. This first blow addled him and slowed his reaction time. In the next instant, he slid down the curved stairs. The stairs scraped chunks of skin off his back, ribs, and spine as they ground along the edge of the stairs, leaving a smeared trail of blood behind. Maggie saw his body and limbs stiffen after his head hit. He continued to tumble down the stairs. His stiff-limbed body tumbled, and with his legs now in the air, he rolled again, hitting his face. During this roll, his feet came around again as Maggie saw his head hit more steps, twisting his neck and head nearly parallel to his shoulder. As he toppled farther, his flailing legs went on either side of the bottom-railing column. He was moving pretty fast by the time he came to the bottom. His speed came to zero, however, when the railing column between his legs met his testicles. Had he been more conscious, he might have had a more outward expression of pain when the crushing blow to his genitals occurred. Instead, it was his primordial cortex that responded by evacuating his bowels as a wave of shock went through his body.

Maggie stood paralyzed in her champagne dress and curled hair. She was dressed and ready for a ball but had just watched the father of her unborn child fall down a set of marble stairs. One second he was strutting nakedly down the stairs, and literally one second later, his head was twisted sideways with his legs were in the air, with more stairs and a blow to the privates yet to come. Maggie ran over to him. She wanted to help him, but she knew not to move him.

"Wyatt!" she said with her voice trembling. "Wyatt, can you talk?"

After a moment he let out a faint groan. Maggie touched his hand. His fingers moved and he groaned again.

"Wyatt? Where are you hurting?"

He groaned more and was trying to speak. He also seemed to be waving his left hand. He was waving it for Maggie to go away.

"Wyatt, what is it?"

"I think...I think I shat."

Maggie thought for a moment about what he was saying. She looked up the stairs and saw the streaks of blood from his back and the streak of feces that came out of him after the column hit him in the nuts.

"Yeah, you did," said Maggie.

"Oh!" Wyatt moaned. "Leave me. Leave me for a sec," he said.

"Do you want me to call an ambulance?"

"No. No. Just give me a couple of minutes. Look away!"

"Do you need anything?" she asked.

His wind had come back, and he was speaking more clearly. "Towels," said Wyatt, with a groan of pain.

She stepped over him and went up the stairs into the bathroom. She got four towels and set them beside him. He waved her away again. She walked away from him as he requested. She sat on the couch with her eyes facing away from him as he tried to move. He first tried moving his arms. He could move them, but it hurt in his ribs, especially on the right side. His neck was killing him, and any movement whatsoever made him wince in pain. When he realized he could move his toes, he figured his back was not broken and he was going to make it, but he knew there would be great agony to follow. His first mission after deciding he would survive the fall was to remove the railing column from his groin. He tried to move his legs, but again his ribs would not have it. He leaned over onto his left side, and with his left arm and feet, scooted back from the post, which sent a wave of nausea through him, and he vomited. Maggie heard this.

"My God, Wyatt! You need help!"

"No, I'm okay," he said through a mucous-and-vomit bubble. He scooted back more, which hurt, but it gave him the adrenaline he needed to sit up, which he did. He grabbed a towel gingerly with his right arm and wiped the vomit from his face. He turned his body more so his legs were pointed down the first step. He attempted to stand, but the rib pain was excruciating, and his neck was sending sharp bolts of pain down his spine. He adjusted his body and tried it again. This time he was successful, but it hurt so badly he screamed in pain.

Maggie was still trying to look away as he had asked, but out of the corner of her eye, she saw him stand, which helped her not panic as much. She was still fighting the urge to call paramedics against his wishes.

Wyatt leaned over and grabbed another towel and cleaned his body while holding his breath. With another towel he slowly leaned over and wiped up the streak of stool on the two steps. With the final towel, he wiped up the vomit. He picked up the four towels and tried to stand up straight but nearly fainted. He steadied himself and took a step up and then another. He soon made it back up the stairs and into the shower.

Maggie heard him turn on the water. She went up the stairs and slowly opened the door. He was standing in the shower with the curtains closed. He was not saying anything.

"Are you all right?" she asked. She was not crying anymore but was still worried about him.

"Yes," he said, but his voice was breaking. "I think I have broken some ribs. They kill me when I move my right arm."

"Oh, Wyatt! I'm sorry. What about your back? Do you need stitches? The stairs were a bloody mess."

"I don't know," he said.

"What about your balls? They broke your fall," said Maggie, now trying with all her might not to giggle.

"I have mashed the hell out of them. It hurts to touch them."

"Oh dear," said Maggie as she crept out of the bathroom to breathe so that no laughter could escape within earshot. She thought the whole thing would have been uproarious, except that he was hurt so badly and would miss the auction because he hurt to move.

"Do you want me to call Marcel for you?"

"Why?" asked Wyatt.

"To tell him you've gotten hurt and won't make it," she said.

"No!" he said, but he groaned as the quick expression rattled the ribs, causing great pain. "I will be there!"

"Wyatt, you can hardly move! There is no way you can go!"

"I'm going!"

"Your bleeding back is a mess, and I'm not sure you didn't break your neck from what I saw!"

"You saw me fall?"

"Yes," she said as a single giggle came out. Wyatt was sure he heard the giggle but ignored it. He knew she could be a bit susceptible to slapstick and bathroom humor.

"What happened?" he asked. Maggie knew she could not hold the laughter if she had to retell the story.

"Well," she started. "You were kind of dancing down the stairs naked..."

"I had a towel!" Wyatt interjected.

"You were kind of dancing down the stairs in nothing but a towel, and your feet slipped." Maggie hoped this would satisfy him, and she would not have to recount more.

"I know that! After that!" he said.

"Well, you...um...tumbled. You hit your head several times and twisted your neck. That was all before you straddled the column and...um...had a little...um...acciden—"

"I get the picture," said Wyatt, now humiliated and in pain. Maggie was glad he wanted to avoid discussing it as she was fighting laughter more than ever. The episode became more hilarious to her every time she replayed it in her mind. Now that she knew he hadn't broken his neck or cracked his skull, she found it even funnier.

"Do you think you can walk?" she asked.

"Yes," he said, turning off the shower. He pulled back the curtain. He was standing straight up with his face forward as that was the position of least discomfort. Maggie handed him a towel. He grabbed it with his left hand and began drying off slowly. Maggie saw that his back was abraded but was not cut deeply. He took the towel and wrapped it around his waist, just as he had done before the fall, but he moved much more cautiously this time. His feet were still slick on the damp marble stairs but he took each step carefully as any sudden movement was painful. Maggie saw that he could at least negotiate the stairs by himself. She held her jokes about "the accident," for now.

Wyatt seemed positive that he was going to the auction, which was to start in an hour. Maggie, still in her dress, handed him his underwear and a T-shirt. He put them on slowly and winced when he had to raise his right arm. When he put on the T-shirt, blood spots came through immediately from his back. She then handed him his tuxedo trousers, and he put them on. He conceded to sit on the bed and allowed Maggie to put his shoes on him. After he had his shoes on, he stood, and Maggie helped him with his cummerbund and tie. After this, he sat on the firm sofa to catch his breath. Maggie also went back upstairs to straighten herself out and see if she had gotten blood—or poo, for that matter—on her dress.

As Wyatt sat on the sofa, he thought about missing the auction. Maybe Marcel would understand. But no, Wyatt would keep his word at all costs and be there. When the time came to go, Wyatt stood again, and Maggie helped him put on his jacket and comb his hair. Maggie saw that the blood had now leaked through to his white shirt, but it was not visible under the jacket. Maggie opened the door and held it open for him. He began walking. The pain was nearly unbearable at first, but as he went farther and walked more normally, the pain subsided slightly for a moment. He figured as long as he stood up very straight and did not move his right arm, he would be fine. Shaking hands was going to hurt. Also turning his head left or right, or any other side movement, sent sharp pains into his muscles.

They walked down the long hall to the ballroom. When they walked in, the three lots that were to sell were set up on displays with elaborate lighting. In the middle of the room was a small stage and podium. The first item was a painting of a simpleton with a feather in his hat. It was painted by Johannes Vermeer in 1650 or so and had recently been found in some Nazi loot. It had been returned to the family, but the family was in dire straits and needed to sell it. Next to that was a small three-foot-tall marble statue of Roman origin with its arms broken off and other items repaired. Then finally, on black velvet under lights, were the three Tricentennial Royals.

The buyers and bidders were beginning to arrive. The sale was to start in forty-five minutes. Marcel was on point in his finest suit, greeting everyone who came. When he saw Wyatt and Maggie enter, he walked over to them.

"Well, it is going okay so far," said Marcel. He was anxious, and asked Wyatt and Maggie to stand near the coins so bidders could ask them questions.

Wyatt nodded without telling him about his injuries.

A few minutes later, Marcel was walking with a finely dressed gentleman and lady in a blue, pearlescent dress. Wyatt heard them talking as they came over.

"Oh, yes, they are amazing! And here are Wyatt and Maggie Mashburn, who found them. Quite a remarkable story," said Marcel to the finely dressed man. Marcel had forgotten Wyatt and Maggie were not married.

"How on earth did you ever find such a thing?" said the man to Wyatt.

"We stumbled upon a letter that alluded to it, so we looked and there they were," said Wyatt with all his effort spent on not groaning or wincing. Maggie stood next to him as he seemed to be on the verge of falling.

"Just there in the ground for all those years," continued the man.

"That's right," said Maggie hoping to save Wyatt some agony. Maggie fought past her usual shyness and did her best to speak for Wyatt, knowing he was in misery.

"Extraordinary!" said the man. Marcel looked at Wyatt and Maggie and nodded with approval. They were playing the part Marcel needed them to play. Wyatt and Maggie did this routine four other times when Marcel was chatting up a patron. They usually asked some question about how they were found, instead of who they were from or who put them there. Each time Maggie gave a delightful answer. Wyatt gave cordial but short answers in a matter-of-fact way that usually intrigued the listener. Wyatt's short sentences and straight posture gave him an air of mystery, which is just what Marcel wanted him to do. Maggie's elegance and sparkle charmed the auction goers she spoke to. She grew more courageous as she spoke to more people.

Soon the crowd had grown dense, and the auction was about to begin. A silver-haired auctioneer in a gray tuxedo announced that the bidding for the Vermeer would begin soon, and everyone gathered around the painting. The auctioneer read the description of the painting and details about how it was last seen in the 1920s but then disappeared until a few years ago when it was found and returned. Wyatt took the opportunity to sit in a chair and rest as they began the bidding. Maggie brought him a glass of water and asked how he was doing as the auctioneer was shouting out numbers.

"Five hundred thousand!" shouted the auctioneer, recording the first bid. More numbers followed. Soon the bidding was at a million and was still going on, but it was slowing down to a duel between two couples. The bidding was at $1.5 million and the bidding increments were getting smaller.

"Going once! Going twice! Sold to the lady and gentleman from Texas," said the auctioneer. "The Vermeer goes for one point seven five million." Thunderous applause came after the announcement.

A few minutes later, the auctioneer began to make announcements about the statue. It was a very fine specimen, according to the statement read by the auctioneer. It was a sculpture in marble by an unknown master of an unknown Roman officer. The bidding started at $100,000 and took a moment to catch the interest of the bidders but was soon at $200,000. The bids were not coming as quickly now. Finally, $300,000 came. Wyatt still sat in the chair, trying not to breathe deeply.

"Sold for three hundred and twenty thousand," said the auctioneer, to more applause.

Now the auctioneer moved toward the Tricentennials. Wyatt stood while Maggie held his arm to steady him as the auctioneer began to speak. "And now, ladies and gentlemen, from Mr. Marcel Duprée and European Antiquities, we have three rare Spanish coins," said the auctioneer. The crowd clapped, and Marcel bowed graciously. "Three Tricentennial Royals, gold coins minted for the king of Spain in 1714. What an interesting story these little jewels must hold. Misplaced in the fray of the Battle of New Orleans, these were found near New Orleans by a regional researcher. They have been authenticated, and we will start the bidding."

Marcel's face turned very grim as the bidding started.

"Do I hear five hundred thousand?" After a moment, he had a bid. "Now six hundred thousand." This kept on for a minute or two until a million was reached. At this point Marcel was able to smile more. The bids went past the $1.1 million point, which marked Marcel's investment. When $1.2 million came, Marcel was all smiles. At $1.375 million, Marcel was gleaming. Finally, "Going, going, *sold*—for one point five two five million to the gentleman from London!" The crowd cheered at the price. Marcel was very happy with his half million in profit, and he began shaking hands with everyone around him. Wyatt stepped back to avoid shaking hands but smiled at Marcel.

The auction was now complete, and the bidders were now in a party mood in the ballroom. The conversations from the crowd of people were filled with laughter and gaiety. Marcel and the auctioneer were up on the stage, smiling for photographs.

Wyatt felt sure he would not be needed much longer and would be able to step out soon. All he wanted to do was to lie down in hopes that the pain in his ribs, back, and neck would abate if he did so. Wyatt was planning on making his exit when he saw the man in a dark suit and with a coiled wire coming from his ear walk into the ballroom. The man was directed toward Marcel. Wyatt saw the man ask Marcel a question. Marcel looked shocked. Wyatt thought he saw Marcel say to the man, "In here?" but he could not be sure. Marcel seemed to be giving permission for something. The man then turned away and left the room. Marcel ran his hand through his hair and walked over to two other gentlemen and informed them of something that was about to happen. The other men looked excited.

Five minutes later, about ten men in black suits poured into the ballroom. They looked to be Secret Service agents. One of them walked up to Marcel and gave him a piece of paper. Marcel immediately walked to the stage and announced to the crowd, "Ladies and gentlemen, the president of the United States of America and the prime minister of Japan!" The crowd gasped and then cheered as everyone turned to see the party enter. Wyatt cared little for politics but recognized the orange-haired man as he walked into the room. He was followed by the smiling Mr. Abe of Japan. The president shook hands with various people who came up to him, but he stayed with Mr. Abe and wanted to show him the items that sold. The crowd followed them as they moved through the room. The president was adding his own personal commentary to the things he showed Mr. Abe. He soon moved to the stage and gestured for Wyatt,

Maggie, and Marcel to come up on stage as they were standing together near the coins, watching. Wyatt did his best to walk up the stairs and stand next to Marcel. Wyatt extended his laft arm in a hook to help Maggie up the stairs. But, it turned into Maggie helping Wyatt up the stairs. Maggie continued to hold Wyatt's arm to steady him as the president approached.

"This is great! Just great! I love it," Trump said to Marcel.

"Thank you, sir. We were very fortunate it worked out in our favor," said Marcel.

"Good to hear!" said Trump. "You just found these?" he asked Marcel.

"No, sir. Wyatt and Maggie found them." Marcel pointed to them and the president turned toward them.

"Ah, a treasure hunter?" Trump said to Wyatt.

"Of sorts, I guess," said Wyatt.

"Good man." Trump reached out and grabbed Wyatt's right hand. He shook it hard. He jerked Wyatt close to him and shook it again. Maggie saw Wyatt turn pale and thought he was going to fall over. He was holding his breath and looking Trump in the eyes.

"This country is great because of ambitious young men like you, Wyatt," Trump said. "You are great! I really mean it!" He shook Wyatt's hand again.

The pain was unbearable. Wyatt had visions of his next humiliation: collapsing while shaking hands with the president. He thought the man had pulled his arm out of its socket. Wyatt squinted his eyes, and they began to water slightly.

Trump took him as a flinty-eyed treasure hunter. He liked him and told him so as he patted Wyatt firmly on the back.

Wyatt thought he was going to vomit from the pain. Trump turned toward Maggie. "Well, Maggie, aren't you lovely," said Trump.

"Thank you," said Maggie.

"So you and this guy, pointing to Wyatt, go around looking for treasures? I love it, and you are very beautiful," said Trump.

Maggie said, "Yes" and "Thank you," not knowing how else to respond to his compliments. Trumped put his arm around Maggie and gave Wyatt and thumbs up.

By now the crowd had gathered around the stage and someone handed the president a microphone. He took it and spoke. "Hello, everyone. We can't stay long. I've just come from upstairs with Mr. Abe, the prime minister of Japan, discussing some very important issues—huge issues that actually we agree on. We heard there were some interesting items down here, and we thought we would pop in to take a look and see all of you."

The crowd cheered as the president waved and smiled. "Hasn't Marcel done a great job arranging all of this? Super! Just super! You are all great Americans, and I want each of you to have a great time tonight!"

With this the crowd cheered again, and he left the stage and headed for the exit with Mr. Abe in tow. Wyatt was concentrating on trying to resume his breathing after having held it.

"Wyatt can you believe it?" said Maggie. "It was really him. He spoke to you and shook your hand."

Wyatt couldn't speak to answer her. He regretted that his fall had ruined their evening. Wyatt saw Maggie's charm, and thought she was beautiful in her gown talking to social elites, but was hurting to badly to join her. Maggie saw that he was going to fall, and she grabbed him to steady him but disguised it as a side hug.

"You want me to get you a chair?" asked Maggie.

"No," he moaned. "Help me back to the room." Maggie kept her arm around him as they turned to walk away from the stage.

"Of all the random things!" said Maggie.

"I know! I thought he was going to kill me! It was all I could do not to puke on him when he jerked my arm."

"This is unbelievable."

"I've got to go to the room. I going to be sick."

When the mass of politicians and security guards left, Maggie took Wyatt back to the room and she helped him lie down and take off his shoes. The next morning his cuts, breaks, and bruises had swollen, and it hurt to move anything. Maggie put the tuxedo and dress back on their hangers so that Robert could pick them up. Wyatt knew they would have to leave the room today and somehow get back to the Silver Beast, which was parked on the edge of the city. He started with sitting up on the side of the bed. It was excruciating. He worked up the strength to stand. His first attempt made him dizzy, so he worked on sitting up straight until he gathered himself enough to try again to rise from the bed.

When he did manage to stand, he stepped slowly around the room, hoping he could loosen up enough to make the trip out of the tower.

He was sitting on a chair a few minutes later when Marcel knocked on the door. Maggie opened it. Marcel was gleaming. The sale had produced a nice profit for him, and he was pleased with the whole venture. The perfect timing of the unexpected appearance of the president had left Marcel euphoric.

"Well, what a trip, huh?" said Marcel as he entered the room.

"Sure was," said Wyatt, still sitting.

"Wyatt, you look rough, you must have had a wild time last night," said Marcel with a smile.

"Sure did," said Wyatt.

Maggie rolled her eyes.

"Well, you deserve it. It's not every day one gets complimented by the president."

"No, I guess not."

"Anyhow, thanks again for coming. The man who bought your coins thought your story was quite remarkable. He was from the British Museum."

"I'm glad it all worked out. Thanks for everything," said Wyatt.

"You bet," said Marcel. "Keep in touch, will you? What are your plans?"

"We are not sure yet. We will drift back south, probably."

"Well, be careful." Marcel walked over and shook Wyatt's hand. He did so with the grace of a gentleman so it did not hurt as badly as Wyatt thought it was going to, and he was able to maintain his composure. Marcel turned to Maggie and smiled while gesturing farewell. "Take care of him."

"I will," said Maggie. With that, Marcel was gone.

Maggie closed the door behind him and turned back to Wyatt. "Why didn't you tell him you nearly broke your neck?" asked Maggie. Wyatt was somewhat appreciative that she summarized the whole episode as "neck breaking," and did not mention the bruised balls or other regrettable details.

"He didn't need to hear all of that."

"You should have told him. He might have helped us get you to the truck."

"I can make it."

"He would not have cared. Accidents happen."

"I did not want to recall the details."

"You could have left those parts out," said Maggie with a giggle.

"We better head out," said Wyatt changing the subject.

Wyatt stood. It hurt, but with one step at a time they left the room and got on the elevator. Maggie stayed close to him as they walked out of the tower and moved slowly toward the subway.

CHAPTER 12

IN THE LINE

———◆———

IN A SHADED MEADOW BY a stream in the Shenandoah Valley sat the Silver Beast. Maggie felt the wind in her hair as the breeze blew her thin dress. She was lost in pleasant reverie. Maggie had driven them from the city to the place they were now. Wyatt sat in the passenger side, writhing in pain from every bump and unexpected turn during the trip. Now he lay still in the camper's bed above the cab. Areas of his skin had developed a patchwork of purple and brown bruises over his back and ribs. His testicles were also bruised and still swollen. He was in misery and did not want to move. The humors leaching from his bruised and swollen tissues caused his mind to whirl. Images and thoughts churned in his head. Ideas and plans quarreled and bickered as to which was the best way and place to find Maggie a house.

As the days passed, his mind became clearer. He thought of himself, as well as his child Maggie was carrying, and what he or she would be like. He thought about his father and brother and what they would be doing now if they were alive.

He wondered how his life would be different from what it was now if his father and brother had lived. Would he have met Maggie, and would they have found the coins? Probably not. He thought about Barbee Collins and imagined him in his place, adventuring through a new frontier and volunteering in Napoleonic era conflicts. He thought about the actions the old man had set in motion two centuries ago and wondered if he had ever pondered the effect his actions would have on a random descendant two hundred years later. Again, probably not. He thought of him sick in a bed as he himself was now, knowing he had put the coins under the foundation stone and needing to get back to retrieve them. Did he put them there under duress? Who in addition to Jackson did he need to hide the knowledge of the coins from? Why didn't he take them with him when he left? Wyatt thought about the descendants of this man who were in the line that led to Wyatt. Wyatt still did not know for sure exactly how he was related to Barbee Collins. He had just taken Uncle Luke's word for it. He did not even know where this accidentally benevolent patriarch was buried. He had never heard of the name Collins before from his family, for that matter. His family had not really spoken of any relatives. He had only met his distant cousins Luke and Charlie recently and quite by chance. This made him think of his life as a giant pinball machine bouncing him from catastrophe to fortune and back again. He felt like his life had just suddenly righted after only drifting. He had some money available now, but in his mind it rightfully belonged to Maggie. Also, the child she carried, was his. This gave him a feeling of lifelong responsibility to her. Why this brought him joy, he did not know.

After nearly a week, he had improved enough that he was able to sit up and move around a bit easier. One evening he was sitting outside in a chair next to Maggie.

"It seems like you are moving better," she said.

"Yes, it is better."

"Your hide is still purple and brown, though."

"Yes, and so are my balls."

"Does it still hurt to pee?"

"No, not too bad."

"When do you think you might want to try to move the rig?"

"I'm about ready," he said.

"There is still no rush. We have time."

"I know, but I've had it on my mind. I'm ready."

"Where are you thinking?"

"I don't know. I think that is the hardest part. I'm okay with anywhere."

"Me too. I can't decide," she said.

"We need an address. My driver's license has the old Flintville address on it. That's where the truck is registered."

"I bet not too many folks find themselves unable to pick a place to live because their choices are unlimited," said Maggie.

"I know. That is kind of odd," said Wyatt.

"We are both still Tennessee residents. You think we should look there first?"

"Sure, I guess. That is fine with me," he said. Wyatt thought awhile longer and remembered some of the places along the way that he thought were beautiful. "What about Flagstaff?"

"It sure was beautiful," she said. "If Marcel had not called, we might still be there."

"That is a long way from here, though. But I guess that doesn't matter," he said.

"No, I guess it doesn't. There is always the Yukon up there with Alex," said Maggie with a pretend shiver.

"I believe I will have to pass on that one. Gwitch'ins may not freeze, but Mashburns do!" This made Maggie smile.

"Wyatt, when you close your eyes and dream of the three of us, what does it look like?"

"I do know the answer to that. I know what that looks like. It has floated in and out a hundred times while I was lying in the camper, trying not to move for the last few days."

"Well, what does it look like?"

"It's green. The yard is green with green trees. A small house with flowers next to the porch."

"That sounds nice. Is it in a town?"

"No, I don't think so. No neighbors in the vision."

"Where do we find that?"

"I don't know, but it is time to look."

Two days later they were on the road. They had stopped at a library in Knox County, Tennessee, for one of their typical research stops. They sat side by side, looking at a computer screen of houses for sale in Tennessee. The volume of choices, prices, colors, and sizes was overwhelming. Finding nothing that gave them a warm feeling, they paused for a break. Wyatt recalled more of the visions that had come to him in the camper a few days ago.

"Look up Barbee Collins," said Wyatt. Maggie typed it in. Sure enough, the results showed he was a captain in Metcalf's First Regiment of Tennessee Volunteers. It was an interesting read. It made Wyatt's mental image of the man more vivid. "What is that part about burial?" Maggie opened it.

"Franklin County, Tennessee," said Maggie.

"That is where he is buried?"

"Yes, that's what it says. There is a map with the cemetery marked."

Wyatt looked at it. "I have never been to Franklin County that I know of," he said.

"Me neither," said Maggie. Maggie went back to the page with houses for sale and narrowed the search to Franklin County. "These are very pretty."

Wyatt thought the reasoning a tad random but the next day found them crossing the picturesque Monteagle Mountain and driving through the pastures and communities around Tims Ford Lake. It was very pretty, even in the brown Tennessee winter. Perhaps it was because they were finally able to contemplate settling temporarily, or maybe it was the beauty of the place, but they did feel a certain connection to the area and found it hospitable and welcoming.

The area around Tims Ford Lake was conducive to easy staging of the Silver Beast for daily excursions into the countryside and finding the houses that Maggie had seen for sale. After only a couple of days, they found a small, quaint, two-bedroom house set upon a hill. It had a small workshop and barn. It was surrounded by a cow pasture from a neighboring farm and had two large ash trees in the front yard that would provide evening shade in the summer. It was beautiful inside. When they looked at it, Maggie filled the rooms in her imagination and saw her life unfolding in this house that could soon be theirs. As they stood together inside of the house, looking out the windows together, they found something to desire.

A month later the Silver Beast pulled alongside a field of knee-high corn sprouts. In the middle of the cornfield was a patch of trees that could be seen from the road. Few knew why the patch of trees existed among the acres of plowed fields until they walked up to it to see the series of graves in the trees. This was the graveyard belonging to Barbee Collins that corresponded to the red dot on the map that Maggie had found. Wyatt and Maggie had taken this opportunity to visit the graveyard to pass some time and pacify their excitement. They were preparing to close on and take possession of the small white house the next day. Furthermore, they had just returned from the doctor to discuss Maggie's ultrasound results. Thus, their minds were afire, and Wyatt suggested they drive out and try to find the grave of Barbee Collins.

The drive was a good distraction from their excitement. They were listening to the last of *Don Quixote* while they drove. They found themselves not able to relate to the man from La Mancha as well as they once had. Sure, calamity had pestered them but it no longer typified them. Quixote's story was woeful but Wyatt and Maggie's was now victorious.

When the Beast came to a stop, Maggie pointed out the tuft of trees in the distance. They got out and walked through the cornfield hand in hand until they arrived at the line of stones in the trees. The largest gray stone in the middle of the others bore the name of Barbee Collins.

"There he is," said Wyatt.

Maggie read the inscription: "Hero of the Battle of New Orleans. Born 1774 and died 1843."

"Someone knew him well enough to put that on his stone," said Wyatt.

"Yep, but I bet they didn't know he had a secret," said Maggie.

"Heck, he may have forgotten it himself."

"Maybe," she said. "I guess he did us a pretty big favor."

"Yes, I guess he did." They stood silently together. Maggie was holding Wyatt's hand.

"Are you excited about the ultrasound?" asked Maggie.

"Yes, I would have been happy with anything, but in truth I am happy this one is a boy."

"Me too," she said.

"That and the house. I can't quit thinking about it."

Maggie could not either, and it made her cry. She was thankful for the way things had turned out. She held on to Wyatt's arm as her lips trembled and a tear rolled down her cheek. After a moment they began walking back to the Silver Beast.

"What do you think about Barbee as a boy's name?" asked Maggie.

"It would be good to name him after a relative, I guess, but Barbee is kind of an odd name for a boy."

"Yes, I was thinking it would be a little odd for nowadays."

They walked back to the truck and got in. They needed something else to do for the rest of the day.

"What do you want to do now?" asked Maggie as her eyes still shone with tears of joy.

"Let's go get married," said Wyatt.

Maggie gave no objections.

THE END

67686911R00157

Made in the USA
Lexington, KY
18 September 2017